"You Want To Be Let Out Of Your Deal With Perfect Match."

"Yes—"

Her stomach plummeted.

"I mean, no." He shook his head.

Her stomach plunged further. It was crazy. She both did and didn't want him as a client. At the same time, at the back of her mind she noted she'd never seen Matt Whittaker so frustrated.

"I don't want to date Bethany or Melanie or Valerie," he said flatly.

"We've already established that."

"I don't want to date women you think your ex would have liked to marry." His eyes met hers. "I want you."

Dear Reader,

I've always been fascinated by the job of matchmakers. As someone who didn't marry until thirty-one, I know just how hard it can be to meet someone special after leaving school.

I hope you enjoy reading Lauren and Matt's story, the last of four books about the Whittaker siblings. When Boston's most eligible bachelor encounters a woman from his past who's a professional matchmaker, will she make a perfect match for him? Can a jilted bride who leads with her heart possibly find happiness with her former ex's groomsman, a tough and enigmatic business tycoon?

Happy reading!

Warmly,

Anna

CAPTIVATED
BY THE
TYCOON

ANNA DePALO

Silhouette®

Desire

Published by Silhouette Books

America's Publisher of Contemporary Romance

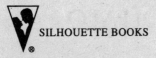 SILHOUETTE BOOKS

ISBN-13: 978-0-373-76775-5
ISBN-10:   0-373-76775-7

CAPTIVATED BY THE TYCOON

Books by Anna DePalo

Silhouette Desire

Having the Tycoon's Baby #1530
Under the Tycoon's Protection #1643
Tycoon Takes Revenge #1697
Cause for Scandal #1711
Captivated by the Tycoon #1775

ANNA DEPALO

Anna discovered she was a writer at heart when she realized most people don't walk around with a full cast of characters in their heads. She has lived in Italy and England, learned to speak French, graduated from Harvard, earned graduate degrees in political science and law, forgotten how to speak French and married her own dashing hero.

A former intellectual property attorney, Anna lives with her husband and son in New York City. Her books have consistently hit the Waldenbooks bestseller list and Nielsen BookScan's list of Top 100 bestselling romances. Her books have won the *Romantic Times BOOKreviews* Reviewers' Choice Award for Best First Series Romance and have been published in over a dozen countries. Readers are invited to surf to www.desireauthors.com and can also visit Anna at www.annadepalo.com.

For Nicholas

One

He was the last man she *wanted* to see. The last man she *expected* to see in her reception room. Matthew Whittaker was heir to one of Boston's great fortunes *and* witness to the most humiliating day of her life.

Lauren came to a halt inside the discreet office doors of Ideal Match. She was unaccustomedly late, thanks to a luncheon appointment that had run overtime and the snow flurries of the uncooperative January weather. Hurried and breathless, she fought to slow her breath as her eyes connected with *his*.

He was already unfurling himself from his position on the couch, and she steeled herself against his looming presence.

"Your two o'clock appointment is here."

Her gaze cut across the reception room to Candace, who raised her eyebrows and opened her eyes wide, then back to the man who stood facing her.

Stalling for time to regain her composure, she slowly walked toward him. "Matt," she acknowledged, relieved that her voice sounded close to normal. "This is a surprise."

"Hello, Lauren," he said. "It's been a while."

When she'd last seen him, he'd been wearing a black tuxedo with a boutonniere of stephanotis. The stephanotis had had fake pearls threaded through their centers, just as she'd requested. It had been *her* wedding, after all.

The look in his blue-velvet eyes on that day five years ago had been unsettling, but then she'd always found him disconcerting.

Her high-heeled pumps sounded on the wood floor before they hit the faux Oriental rug covering the center of the reception area. She kept a professional smile on her face as she reached him. "It's lovely to see you again."

As her outstretched hand was engulfed in his, she quelled the little flutter of sensation in her midriff.

"I thought it might be," he said with a wry smile. After a beat, he added, "A surprise, that is."

Looking up at him, she had a ringing reminder of her small stature. Even in heels, she qualified as petite—a fact she'd been ruing for all of her thirty years.

Young, short and female. A winning combination for being taken seriously by any yardstick.

He, on the other hand, had everything going for him. At least six feet, he was also wealthy, male and imposing. Hadn't she read somewhere that the height of a candidate was a better predictor of who would win a Presidential election than almost any other factor?

She swept him a look from beneath her lashes. He had the dark good looks of a *GQ* model, but he was also—what was the word she was searching for?— *enigmatic.*

She recalled the recent *Fortune* magazine cover story about him. He'd been called the financial engineer of Whittaker Enterprises because of his cool, unflappable style as CFO of the aggressively competitive family conglomerate.

Ironically, the *Boston Sentinel* had also named him Boston's Most Eligible Bachelor for two years running. After his younger brother, Noah, had gotten married, Matt had succeeded to the title almost by default.

Still, surely he wasn't here for her matchmaking services. Yet, what other explanation was there? He was her two o'clock.

As if on cue, he said, "I've got to be the last person you expected to see as a client."

Please God, no. No, no, no. Not him. Not the man who'd remained perplexingly impassive in the face of her abject humiliation five years ago. Not the man who perversely made her acutely aware of her femininity.

Collecting herself, she nodded to Candace, then said smoothly, "Won't you come in? We'll be able to talk at length in my office about what you're looking for and how we can help you find it." She mentally winced—it wasn't as if he was looking to be matched to a computer or some other emotionless object, much as she might think it appropriate. "I mean *her.*"

His eyes showed a flicker of an emotion suspiciously like amusement.

When he'd followed her into her office, she shut the door behind them, shooting a frown at her receptionist, who wore an openly curious expression.

Taking off her coat, she waved him to a seat. As she walked over to a cabinet set along one wall, she asked, "Tea? Coffee?"

"No, thanks."

She felt like a fortifying gulp of something strong and caffeinated herself. Instead, she reluctantly retraced her steps and sat down in an armchair at a right angle to his seat on the couch.

She watched as he glanced around her office, looking about as comfortable as a caged panther. She waited for him to get to the point.

Finally, his gaze came back to hers. "My sister and sisters-in-law think the world would be a better place if I were as happily married as they all are."

She waited.

"My sister suggested hiring you."

She moved forward in her seat. "I'm afraid I only take on clients who are sure—"

"I've decided she may be right."

Oh. She inched back in her chair, then tried again. "Since you've been dubbed Boston's Most Eligible Bachelor, I don't see why you'd need to hire a matchmaker. The title alone—"

"Heard about it, have you?" he asked sardonically.

"Yes," she admitted. "I read the *Sentinel,* and anyway, it's my business to know who the eligible singles are in this town."

"That's just it." He raked his hand through his hair. "That ridiculous title makes me the target of every gold digger and social climber around. Being named Boston's Most Eligible Bachelor *once* was bad enough, but now that I've had the title two years running, it's getting to be more than merely irritating. I've seen my brothers targeted by unscrupulous women, and I've got no desire to be part of a repeat performance." He paused. "That's where you come in."

"It's one thing to want to avoid unscrupulous women, it's another to want to find a meaningful relationship."

"I'm thirty-six. It's time."

"Time?"

He gave a curt nod. "I've spent the past decade putting in long hours in the boardroom, but I don't want to be sixty by the time my kids hit Little League."

He made it sound so methodical. *So logical,* she thought.

"Besides," he went on, "I don't have the time to

take a scattershot approach. I'm counting on finding the right woman by the time the *Sentinel* gets around to naming its Most Eligible Bachelor again three months from now."

He was seeking her out, Lauren thought, for the same reason a lot of her high-powered clients did. Neither he nor they had the time to take a casual approach to finding Mr. or Ms. Right. And with their type A personalities, they thought finding the right mate could be approached in the same way as they did everything else in their lives—throw some money at the problem and hire someone to do the legwork.

She supposed she shouldn't be surprised a corporate mogul like Matt would think he could tackle finding a wife in the same way.

"Hiring a matchmaker isn't a quick-fix solution," she warned. "My clients sometimes forget they still need to commit time, effort and emotional energy to nourish a relationship."

He nodded. "Understood. I'll make the time, but I'll rely on *you* to make it worth it." After a pause, he added, "There'll be excellent publicity for Ideal Match if you pair off Boston's Most Eligible Bachelor."

He had a point there. Naturally, astute businessman that he was, he couldn't resist pointing out the bottom-line benefits of taking him on as a client.

Parker, her ex-fiancé, had been the same way. Of course, since Matt and Parker had been buddies at

Harvard Business School, it wasn't surprising there were other similarities between them.

She, on the other hand, was a walking billboard for making business decisions with her heart and not her head. Fortunately, she'd chosen a field where that kind of thinking was rewarded. Still, she was probably the only matchmaker in the city of Boston who took on charity cases, thanks to her volunteer work at a senior citizens' retirement community.

Yet, if she succeeded in pairing Matt off with Ms. Right, Ideal Match would be vaulted to a whole new level of visibility. It would be a major coup, in fact. So what if Matthew Whittaker was an ever-present reminder she was a phony whose fiancé had jilted her and whose personal experience of passion and love everlasting was nil?

She thought again about how much taking on Matt would help her business. Surely she could handle him. She'd held her own against difficult CEOs who were too busy to follow up on dates, pompous perfectionists who thought they were God's gift to women, and even teary-eyed prima donnas who'd been planning their weddings in the womb.

She watched now as Matt looked around her office.

Ideal Match was located in one of downtown Boston's sleek new office towers. Most of her clients were busy professionals who not only expected a certain image from her business, but ease of accessibility, as well.

But while the building was sleek and new, she'd tried hard to make Ideal Match's offices comfy and inviting. The decorating scheme was dark woods dressed in maroons and browns and highlighted with creams and some gold.

"You've been doing well for yourself," he said finally, his eyes coming back to hers. "When did you start Ideal Match?"

"Over four years ago. You'd be surprised at how much a flawless diamond engagement ring can fetch at a pawnshop."

The words were out of her mouth before she could stop them. Had he expected her to crawl into a hole five years ago and refuse to emerge? She had been tempted to run back to California and her family's comforting embrace, but she'd resisted the urge.

He cocked his head and regarded her steadily. "No, I'm not surprised," he murmured, before adding more distinctly, "I'm glad the past few years have been good for you."

She limited herself to thanking him politely, because the last thing she wanted was to revisit that fateful day with him.

Hers was supposed to have been the perfect June wedding. Even the weather had cooperated. It had been sunny and warm. But aside from the weather, nothing had gone as planned.

Growing up, she'd always been afraid that if she threw a party, it would be a flop. Her wedding was supposed to have been the biggest party she'd ever hosted but instead it had been her worst nightmare.

Still, even when things had gone awry, nothing had followed a trite script. The groom hadn't run off, leaving his best man to give the bride the bad news. Instead, Parker had come himself. And, she hadn't fallen into a fit of tears. Instead, she'd squared her shoulders and gone on with the party.

She'd been adjusting her veil in her hotel suite when Parker had appeared, saying they needed to talk. The rest had played like a head-on collision in slow motion: she could see it coming, but she was powerless to do anything about it. He was calling off the wedding…things just didn't feel right…he had some more living to do…sorry for hurting her.

She'd just stared at Parker, watching the words come out of his mouth but unable to react because of the paralyzing shock gripping her.

He hadn't even had the decency to tell her his news the night before, at the rehearsal dinner, *before* nearly one hundred fifty wedding guests were packing the church, lining the aisle she was supposed to walk down in the next hour.

And then her eyes had slid to Matt, who'd appeared behind Parker. He'd been dressed in groomsman's attire, but the look on his face had been stony and forbidding. If she'd been seeking a shoulder to cry on, *his* was obviously not available.

Ironically, his reaction had fortified her. An announcement had been made to the guests, and then with head held high, she'd gone on with the reception—this time as a salute to the wedding that wasn't. The guests had admired her pluck, but only she knew how devastating it had been to take off for her honeymoon with her maid of honor instead of her husband.

And yet, she'd managed to turn adversity on its head. She'd left the matchmaking firm she'd been working for and started her own business. Although she had no desire for a repeat walk down the aisle herself, she believed she'd learned from hard experience how to gauge compatibility.

Pairing up happy couples had helped her heal. She could count multiple marriages among her success stories, and at each ceremony, she'd cried tears of happiness.

"It's still painful for you," Matt said, calling her back from her thoughts.

There wasn't any need for him to elaborate. They both knew what he was talking about. Wanting to change the course of the conversation, she reached over to the coffee table in front of them for the folder Candace had left for her.

Somewhere along the way—and maybe it was just some immature need to prove to him she'd moved on with her life—she'd decided to take him on as a client.

Opening the folder, she said, "So, what are you looking for in a woman?"

You. The answer jumped unbidden into his head. Where the hell had that thought come from?

Matt gave himself a mental shake. He hadn't given much thought to putting into words what he was looking for in a woman.

Aloud he said, testing, "Down-to-earth."

"Anything else?"

He thought for a moment. "Stylish."

He noticed *she* wore a black V-neck top over a slim gray skirt and high-heeled black leather boots. Her jewelry was simple—just hoop earrings, a watch and a lariat necklace.

She looked over the questionnaire he'd filled out in the reception area, then glanced up, frowning. "You didn't respond to all of the questions here."

He gave an unapologetic shrug.

She tossed him a disapproving look before going back to the form in front of her.

As Lauren continued to look over his printed answers, Matt reflected on the restless feeling he'd been unable to shake off. He'd kept his nose to the grindstone for the past decade, building up his business ventures, both in his role as Chief Financial Officer of Whittaker Enterprises and for his own private investment.

These days, though, he felt like the odd man out at family gatherings with his siblings. Quentin had married interior designer Elizabeth Donovan and become father to a baby boy. Then Allison had married Connor Rafferty, Quentin's old college buddy. And not too long after that, Noah had tied the knot with Kayla Jones, who'd been Ms. Rumor-Has-It for the *Sentinel*'s gossip page.

The more he'd thought about it, the more hiring a matchmaker made sense—particularly since, as long as the *Sentinel* continued to bestow its ridiculous title on him, every shrewd, fortune-hunting female in the greater Boston area would be pursuing him with a vengeance.

It couldn't hurt to give Lauren's service a shot for a few months. His time was valuable, and though he couldn't change the past, Lauren's business would get a boost if she could claim to have paired off Boston's Most Eligible Bachelor.

Just then Lauren looked up from reviewing the questionnaire, calling him back from his thoughts.

Pen poised over paper, she said briskly, "Let's fill in the blanks."

He almost smiled at her business-like tone.

"Do you have a preferred hair color?"

He looked at her hair. "I like brunettes."

Her hair had a silky, smooth look to it and fell past her shoulders. He was glad she hadn't cut it since he'd last seen her. It appeared even longer than he remembered it being.

"Age range?" she asked, looking up from jotting down his first answer.

"Someone in her thirties." He tried to remember how old she'd been at the time of her wedding five years ago. Twenty-five?

She pinned him with a penetrating look. "Would you date someone who's older than you are?"

The corner of his mouth lifted. "I'm an equal opportunity dater."

His droll humor was met with more scribbling. "Eye color?"

Her eyes were the lovely blue-green of the sea. It was one of the first things he'd noticed about her when Parker had introduced her to him as his fiancée five years ago. Aloud, he heard himself say, "Doesn't matter, but I'm partial to green."

"Height?"

He eyeballed her. Even though she was sitting down, he estimated she couldn't be more than five foot five or six, even in heels. Tall enough for him, he figured. "Not too tall."

She looked at him skeptically. "You're over six feet. Are you sure you want to date petite women?"

Oh, yeah, he thought. And, kiss them, too, if their lips were anything like hers: full and beckoning.

He reined in his wayward thoughts. He wasn't here to date Lauren, he was here to hire her. She was just a good model for what he *might* find attractive in a woman, considering he hadn't given it much thought before showing up for this appointment. He knew what he *didn't* want, and as for the rest, he'd know it when he saw her.

Aloud he said, "I've dated petite women in the past." It was a bit of a stretch. "It's not an issue for me."

She arched an eyebrow.

He looked back at her blandly.

After a moment, she jotted down his answer and his others to her subsequent questions, then set her pad aside.

She crossed and then uncrossed her legs.

He waited.

She cleared her throat. "One of the things I've learned from running this business for the past four years is that, to *make* an ideal match, I often have to prepare my client to *be* an ideal match."

He wondered where this conversation was heading.

"What I mean is," she continued, apparently choosing her words with care, "sometimes people, no matter how successful in their professional lives, need a few pointers."

"Cut to the chase." In his business dealings, he was used to laying out what needed to be said, without hedging or apologies.

She shifted. "I've seen the occasional press about you. You're described as cool, calculating and aloof."

He was proud of those characteristics, he wanted to tell her. They kept his business adversaries off balance, just the way he liked them. Still, while he might be like that publicly, privately was a different matter—at least when he wasn't around her. Five years ago, he'd had a frustrating inability to get beyond stiff conversation with her.

"Ideal Match can help," she went on quickly. "Before turning you loose on a real date, we can work on the total package together."

"The total package?" he prompted.

She nodded. "Creating your best *you*. Clothes, image, conversation skills…"

She waved her hand in the air as if further explanation was unnecessary.

Matt recalled that Allison had said Lauren was called Dr. Date. Now he knew why—besides the fact she'd had more than a few success stories with her services. "So you're going to coach me?"

A fleeting look of discomfort crossed her face, then she said crisply, "Something like that."

"Fine." He was used to making fast decisions. It was the only way to survive when you swam with the corporate sharks. Besides, he could afford to pay her well for her services.

And then, of course, Ms. Matchmaker might discover there were a few lessons that *he* could teach *her.*

Two

Luxurious. The word flashed again through Lauren's mind as she stepped into the elevator of Matt's building.

The doorman had already announced her arrival. She'd heard Matt's voice through the phone instructing the uniformed doorman to show her up.

She made a mental note to herself that Matt apparently didn't retain a housekeeper on weekends. She'd learned long ago that every bit of information about a client could prove useful in constructing a profile for his ideal match.

They'd agreed to meet at his apartment on a Saturday—the only time Matt had available—to begin figuring out how to package him to meet Ms. Right.

As the elevator rose, its wood paneling and Oriental-pattern carpeting adding to the ambience of a building that spoke of wealth in hushed tones, Lauren wondered again whether she'd been crazy to take on this assignment.

Her effectiveness as a matchmaker depended on her ability to keep an emotional distance from her clients, but Matt was associated with the most explosive drama of her life.

On top of it all, she'd long ago sworn off on anybody associated with her former fiancé. Matt was rich, privileged and born to rule, and he'd been Parker's would-be groomsman. In her mind, they were cut from the same cloth.

In fact, the building she'd just entered was the type of place she'd envisioned Matt living in. It was dark brick and prewar, with liveried doormen and a dark green awning.

The Whittakers were old-line, old-money Boston. Not surprisingly then, Matt's apartment wasn't a pretentious sprawling penthouse in a gleaming new high-rise, with an elevator opening directly into the apartment.

Instead, as she discovered when the elevator doors opened, there were two apartments on the top floor, and they shared a softly lit hallway.

Matt stood in the doorway to his apartment. He was dressed in business clothes, minus the suit jacket and tie.

He stepped aside. "Come on in. You're right on time."

Her heart beat faster. He was big, male and coated with just a veneer of civility.

Irritated with her reaction, she said, "Because we all know time is money, don't we?"

Moving past him into the apartment, she added, "That's the last impression you want to convey to a date."

He followed her in and closed the door. "But what if I am timing her?"

"Maybe it would be best to save that sort of thing for after the wedding." She knew it sounded as if they were talking about kinky sex, but proper dating etiquette *was* important in her book.

He made a sound of disbelief. "All right, duly noted. A patient guy may be the ultimate female fantasy, but he *is* just a fantasy."

She smiled encouragingly. "Well, when we're done, hopefully *you'll* be the ultimate female fantasy."

And, judging from the way her body was humming, he wasn't doing a half-bad job as it was.

"I'll start right now by taking your coat," he said smoothly.

"Thank you."

The brush of fingers at the nape of her neck sent shivers chasing down her spine.

After depositing her coat in a closet, he said, "Let me show you around."

She tried to quell the spine-tingling sensations as he gave her a brief tour of the apartment.

The kitchen was spacious, with glass-door cherrywood cabinets, a large marble-topped center island and Miele stainless steel appliances.

In the formal dining room, the walls were painted red above ivory wainscoting and below ivory-painted molding. The chairs were upholstered in red and gold stripes, and several pieces, including the sideboard, looked as if they were antiques.

Lauren couldn't help contrasting Matt's dining room with the modest one in the home in Sacramento she'd grown up in, where the chintz wallpaper had been put up by her mother and the furniture bore the dents and scratches of one too many feet, including hers and those of her younger sister and brother.

When they moved on to Matt's living room, she noted that this room at least was a nod to comfort. Sofas and armchairs, dressed in beige fabric and chocolate leather, clustered around a large fireplace.

The den followed on from the living room. Built-in bookshelves lined two walls, while the windows showcased spectacular views of downtown Boston.

Lauren could tell this was where Matt spent most of his time. The desk was covered with piles of paper and documents, and a laptop lay open. It was the only room so far that contained a trace of disorder.

Finally, they came to a long hallway.

Matt nodded down the rug-covered expanse. "This leads to the bedrooms and baths. A couple of years ago, I had the option to buy the apartment below and make this place into a duplex with a guest wing on the lower floor." He shrugged. "But the apartment was already more than big enough for a bachelor."

"Yes, I see."

The penthouse was masculine and understated, but bore the unmistakable markings of a professional designer's hand. Still, for all the expense, there was something missing.

It took her a second to figure out what.

There was no warmth to the place. No photographs documenting the occupant's major life moments, no collectibles from memorable vacations, not even awards hinting at hobbies and favorite pastimes.

In short, Matt Whittaker remained as much a cipher as ever.

"It may need a little helping hand, however," she said slowly.

"What does?"

"Your apartment."

He looked around and frowned. "What's wrong with it? I paid a professional."

"Exactly."

"It cost plenty—"

"—but has no heart," she finished for him. "I'm surprised your designer didn't incorporate your mementos and prized possessions when she redecorated."

"The designer was someone recommended by my sister-in-law, and she did. But my stuff is still boxed up."

"Hmm…and how long ago did you redecorate?"

He did not look amused. "I do a lot of corporate travel. I'm rarely here."

"If you don't have time to live in your apartment, you won't have time to call her for a date."

He looked ready with a rebuttal, and she restrained herself from tsk-tsking at the forbidding expression on his face.

"The deadline is Wednesday, by the way."

"Wednesday, for what?"

"The day of the week by which you'll call her for a weekend date."

She realized she sounded like a scolding nanny, but it was the only way she knew not to be overwhelmed by him.

"Got it," he said dryly. "Why do I feel as if I should be taking notes?"

"It may be a good idea. Anyway, traveling frequently would be a good excuse *if* you had another place you called home instead of—" she gestured around her "—this."

He arched a brow.

"I'm not going to redecorate your apartment." She sought to reassure him.

"Happy to hear it."

"But I would suggest a few pieces to give a woman a clue about you. Maybe some strategically placed photos. Nothing major. We can find some frames that blend with your new decor."

She was *not* going to be intimidated by him, she

told herself for the umpteenth time. She'd handled high-powered prosecutors and corporate titans without being unnerved.

"Let's look at your closets next," she heard herself say. "Then maybe we can take the shopping trip we discussed as a possibility for this afternoon."

On to his bedroom. She was about to discover what lay at the end of the long hallway in front of her.

His bedroom was huge, easily the size of half her modest apartment. A king-size bed dominated, and the furniture had a contemporary look—dark with clean lines and brushed metal knobs. A master bath was visible through one open door, and a fireplace occupied the wall facing the bed.

She took a deep breath. The room was as imposing as its occupant, but she was a professional. At least as far as matchmaking went, she qualified to herself.

She looked at the closet on the far wall. "May I?"

"Go right ahead."

When she threw open the double doors, she was confronted by expensive shirts and conservative business suits hanging in neat rows. Everything was a variation on a theme.

"Where's the casual clothing?" She looked at him, then raised a hand to stop him before he could answer. "No, don't tell me. You live in suits most of the time."

He cocked his head. "Very perceptive of you."

"We'll have to fix that."

His look was sardonic. "Do you subject your female clients to this treatment?"

"Absolutely. It's not about becoming someone you're not, but about creating a *better* you."

"So what do you recommend to the women?"

"Now if I told you, I'd be letting you in on the secret handshake."

"My lips are sealed."

She sighed. "I'll share only because I think you'll put this information to good use."

A smile played at his mouth. "I'm all ears."

"Well, I recommend that with clothing, they start with the basics, which *never* go out of fashion. A little black dress, a suit, a pair of jeans, a white shirt, nude color high heels, and a pair of sneakers. As far as jewelry, a watch and pearls."

"You're kidding."

"Why would I joke?" she asked. "The basics are just that. They can be mixed and matched to take you from morning to evening, casual to formal."

"Okay, I have to ask. Why nude on the heels?"

"It's sexy," she said simply. "It draws the eye away from the feet and upward, which makes a woman appear taller, and is particularly important if she's—" she paused, as she belatedly realized how much she was revealing, and finished lamely "—ah, petite."

He gave her a look of mock gravity. "You've thought about this a lot."

"Naturally." He could make fun all he wanted, but she had a nice little business going—and he'd been the one to seek out her help.

He raked her with his eyes, from the faux pearls set off by her scoop-neck sweater and the black jeans hugging her curves to her wedge sandals.

She shifted self-consciously, then gave herself a mental shake.

She was his matchmaker, and she was going to get him married off to some appropriate socialite or wannabe—even if she had to custom order a woman from Mattel with mythical characteristics to match a Barbie doll's mythical proportions.

She *was* going to make him Ideal Match's biggest success story to date, even if it dredged up every single best-forgotten memory in her.

"I suppose the pearls can be fake?" he queried.

"Of course. Everyone knows it's nearly impossible to tell the difference between real and faux pearls by sight alone."

"It's nice to know your 12-step plan is accessible to the masses."

She began flipping through the clothes hanging in his closet. "If you're going to mock it, this exercise isn't going to work."

"Don't worry. I'm taking it *very* seriously." He paused. "So what basics do you advise men to take to a deserted island with them?"

"Prince Charming doesn't need a list of essentials," she said, matching his irreverent tone, "because for men, fashion is all about the basics. You know, suits, ties…a tux."

"Great. Looks like I already have it covered."

"Yes, but a pair of jeans would be useful," she said, glancing back at him. "Men have the opposite problem from women, and that's an inability to move beyond the essentials."

"I own a pair of jeans."

"That are how old—?"

He eyed her. "Nothing much escapes you, I can tell."

She gave him a modest smile. "You hired me, you get the full extent of my expertise."

"All right, how about this?" he countered. "I *like* my jeans, even if I don't get to wear them much these days."

"Yes, I know. Because you do a lot of business travel. We'll need to do something about that. In the meantime, let's get you into something your old college buddies won't recognize."

Lauren hoped if she kept concentrating on the task at hand, she'd keep illicit thoughts at bay. Authority and male power clung to him like a second skin, and she felt diminutive and feminine in contrast.

He looked at her bemusedly. "You know, I don't let just anyone talk to me this way. Those who work for me never do, and even my business rivals know better."

His look turned thoughtful. "This isn't how I remember you."

"Things can change in a few years," she forced herself to say. She'd vowed never again to be so vulnerable…so naive.

"I can see that."

They were drifting into dangerous territory, so she faced the closet again and tapped her lips with her index finger. "I'm thinking Helmut Lang on the jeans."

"No way."

She glanced at him. "If you were a denim fanatic, I'd suggest Japanese jeans made from organic cotton and natural dyes."

"What's wrong with Levi's?"

"Nothing. It depends on the message you want to send." The thought of him filling out a formfitting pair of Levi's sent a wave of heat through her. "Actually, it wouldn't hurt to inject an element of everyman into your image. It might be a nice balance, particularly if what you said in our interview is true and you're looking for a down-to-earth woman."

"I am."

"All right, then." Her gaze went back to his closet. "Let's see if we can wake things up a bit."

"No."

"Real men wear pink."

Matt eyed the dress shirt in Lauren's hand. "Not flamingo pink."

This afternoon's shopping trip hadn't been

going as he'd expected. They'd hit some of Boston's upscale men's stores, ending up in Neiman Marcus.

As far as Matt could tell, Lauren was intent on softening his hard edges. Her idea appeared to be to make him *seem* like less of a hard-driving business executive so, with any luck, he'd *become* less of one, as well.

Not a chance, he wanted to warn her.

She sighed. "I see I'll have to introduce you to P. Diddy's fashion line."

"Stick to Ralph Lauren Polo. You might have better luck."

"You know, if I really wanted to recommend something trendy, I'd suggest bespoke clothing."

"Bespoke?"

"Handmade."

He made a sound of disbelief. He had his suits custom-made, but hand sewn was a different matter.

"Just for the record, the shade we were talking about is called fiesta berry."

"They can call it lucky gambler's red, but I won't be wearing it."

A middle-aged salesman approached, wearing a polite smile. "May I offer some assistance?"

"Thanks, but we were just leaving."

Lauren smiled apologetically at the clerk. "We're looking for something casual, but we seem to be having a difference of opinion."

The man nodded. "Wives sometimes have a different opinion from their husbands."

A look of embarrassment crossed Lauren's face. "We're not—"

"What my wife is trying to say," he cut in, "is that we're not looking just for casual clothing. She's trying to soften my image at work, too."

Lauren opened her mouth, but before she could say anything more, he took her elbow and steered her toward the salesman. "Come along, sweetheart. Let's see what he can show us."

To the salesclerk, he said, "Let's start with some casual pants."

"Very good," the salesman said. "If you'll follow me…?"

As they walked toward another section of the store, Lauren muttered, "What are you doing? If anyone recognizes you and thinks we're an item, or worse, that you're secretly married, you'll undermine everything we're trying to accomplish."

"Don't worry," he said easily. "I'm the kind of action hero who is invisible to everyone but husband-hunting females."

She gave him a sidelong look. "Really? And your superhero powers would be—?"

"I'd show you, but they're best demonstrated *privately.*"

She compressed her lips. "I don't know why he assumed we're married. Neither of us is wearing a wedding band."

"Not everyone wears a ring. Besides, girlfriends don't pick out a man's clothes, wives do."

She opened her mouth again.

"If he thinks we're married, he'll listen to you. Otherwise, he'll keep addressing me."

"You put me on the spot."

"Learn to ask for what you want. That's the problem with women."

She pulled her elbow from his grasp. "We'll have to work on your unfortunate tendency to put the words *problem* and *women* in the same sentence."

"When have I done that?" he said mildly. Ever since she'd arrived at his apartment, he felt as if he'd been taken to task by Ms. Manners. "All I said was I've been targeted by social climbers and gold diggers."

"Same thing," she responded before giving her attention to the salesman.

Lauren and the clerk got into a conversation about the "it" colors of the season and various private labels.

Matt limited his answers to *yes, no* and *forget it*. It was the way he was used to operating in the boardroom, and the approach had served him well.

He could tell it was exasperating Lauren, however.

When the clerk had gone to try to find an appropriate size, she asked, "Could you volunteer more than one-word answers?"

He gave her a slow smile. "Yes."

She sucked in a breath, causing her chest to rise, and his gaze headed south.

When his eyes met hers again, a momentary but electric pause ensued.

"We may need to work on your conversation skills, too," she said into the silence.

"They've served me well enough in the boardroom. Extraneous words are wasted energy. Why talk when there are more effective ways of communicating?"

He itched with a sudden urge to show her just how effective other modes of communication could be. They were standing in a very public place, with shoppers milling about around them, yet it felt as if they were in their own private world.

The salesman's return, however, broke the spell, and they were directed toward a changing room. Lauren was shown to a chair outside to wait.

In the private room, he shrugged out of his clothes and into a pair of khakis and a casual shirt. He emerged a few minutes later so Lauren could pass judgment.

"Hmm," she said.

Sitting with legs crossed, she tilted her head to the side. "Turn around."

He eyed her, then did as she asked. The clothes weren't his usual style but he was willing to bend a little.

More important, he couldn't detect a hint that she was enjoying issuing commands and sitting in judgment. Still, he had his suspicions.

He turned back around.

"Good fit," she said.

He'd never thought two such innocent words could be so erotic.

In fact, this whole shopping trip was turning into a more intimate experience than he'd ever have guessed. He felt like a Chippendales dancer at the start of a routine.

"Are you comfortable?" she asked.

Comfortable wasn't the word he'd use. *Turned-on* was more like it, and if he wasn't careful, it would soon be evident to everyone else, as well.

Aloud, he said, "They fit fine." He nodded at the salesman standing nearby. "We'll take them."

"Very good," the salesman said. "There are some belts I can show you."

When the man had gone, Lauren said, "You're decisive."

"Impatient," he corrected. "Usually I'm in and out of stores like this in less than thirty minutes. Ten to find what I'm looking for, five to try it on for size, and another ten to pay and make it out the door."

She smiled sweetly. "But you're such a natural!"

So she *was* enjoying this.

"I feel like a model in a bad TV ad," he muttered.

"Actually, I'm helping to organize a fashion show to raise money for the Boston Operatic League. We're still short on male volunteers to model the designer clothes that have been donated."

"Forget it."

"Consider it," she cajoled. "It would be a wonderful way to meet people. You'd be in the perfect environment to find some sweet-tempered woman who thinks supporting the arts is important, while promoting yourself in the best light possible by helping out."

"Nice try, but no dice." In fact, if either of his brothers ever got wind of the fact he'd paraded up and down some runway in front of dozens of judgmental women, they'd dissolve into paroxysms of laughter. Not to mention that his reputation as a tough corporate adversary would take a hit.

He needed to slam on the brakes before Lauren transformed him into some smoking-jacket-wearing, charity-auction-volunteering, in-touch-with-his-feelings dream man.

He had his limits.

And those limits apparently included Levi's, which is what he came away with, along with assorted other purchases.

As the salesclerk wrapped up the purchases, Matt admitted to himself that Lauren knew her stuff. If the matchmaking gig didn't work out for her, she had a future as a personal shopper.

He'd let her take control today, more than he'd ever let anyone else do it when it came to his life. Or, rather, she'd alternately cajoled, coaxed and teased her way into getting what she wanted—at least some of the time.

The fact she was so small, and he loomed over her, just added to the irony of it all.

Thinking of how he outsized her, his body tightened, and he had to remind himself again that petite women weren't his usual style. Especially one particular bossy petite woman who acted as if she was unsure whether she liked him. A petite woman whose primary interest in him appeared to be to further her business.

If it were otherwise, he'd have to start asking himself sticky questions about his past motives, and he didn't want to go there.

So naturally, the first words out of his mouth were, "When are you open for dinner so I can brush up on my conversation skills?"

Three

It was just business and dinner. At least that's what Lauren told herself. In fact, however, this practice dinner was unlike any other she'd been on.

Back at her initial meeting with Matt in her office, she'd mentioned she sometimes helped her clients with their conversation skills. She'd almost forgotten the fact...until Matt had decided to sign himself up.

Given how she'd barely survived their shopping outing last weekend, she'd approached tonight with not a little trepidation.

She'd been unable to stop thinking about Matt and how he'd looked on Saturday. The way he'd filled a pair of Levi's...the way his lean muscles had appeared under a smooth T-shirt…the way her pulse had raced in response.

Getting dressed for dinner had been its own special torture. She'd waffled over what to wear.

She had a set repertoire for business meals—clothes that were chic but not too sexy. But hours ago, she'd decided nothing in her closet conveyed the right tone.

She'd finally settled on a wrap dress in a midnight color with three-quarter-length sleeves. She'd kept her hair loose and put on a pair of chandelier earrings. She'd finished off with black pumps.

Sure, it wasn't her usual attire. It was more elegant cocktail party than expensive dinner. Still, her clothes were her armor, and she had to come equipped to handle the client she was seeing—in this case, two-hundred-plus pounds of high-powered male testosterone.

Now they sat facing each other, like two opponents in the centuries-old battle of the sexes, their weapons cutlery, wine goblets and as much repartee as she could stomach over an elegant dinner of lobster *panzerotti*.

They made small talk about their families, and they'd just started a conversation about the local theater scene when, with an apologetic look, Matt reached into his pocket. "I'm getting a call."

He flipped open the phone. "Hello."

Matt's eyes stayed on hers while he listened.

Despite knowing his mind was elsewhere, Lauren

felt tingling awareness dance along her nerve endings, just as it had done throughout dinner. Still, somewhat surprisingly, she'd found herself enjoying their conversation.

She watched as Matt said, "Right, okay."

He flipped the phone closed and placed his table napkin to the side of his plate, his mouth set in a firm line. "I've got to take this."

He got up, and she was distracted from replying by the waiter's arrival to refill their wineglasses.

Ten minutes later, he was back.

As he sat down, she said, "Definitely a no-no."

"Don't tell me," he said with mock warning.

"No cell phone calls. It gives the impression—"

"I know. It gives the impression I work for my money."

"No, that you're a workaholic."

He looked exasperated. "It's a Tuesday night."

"Turn off the phone," she said firmly. "Particularly on the first date."

"This isn't a real date."

His response stung, even though he'd spoken the truth, and she worried again about her difficulty in keeping a professional distance.

Steering the conversation to safer waters, she said, "Why don't you tell me a little bit about your job?"

He raised a brow. "I thought I was supposed to be downplaying the fact that work is my mistress?"

"This isn't a real date, remember?" she echoed,

determined this time to remember the fact herself. "Besides, you need to practice how to leverage your job for maximum appeal on your real dates."

"*Leverage* my job for maximum appeal? Is that matchmaker talk?"

"No, that's what I call the Fletcher Method speaking."

"How about letting my sizable cash flow speak for itself?" he quipped.

"Is that how an accountant talks dirty?" she parried.

He chuckled. "All right, I'll play nice."

Done with his food, he sat back and toyed with the stem of his wineglass.

She tore her mind away from thoughts of his firm, squareish, capable-looking hands.

"You're the Chief Financial Officer of Whittaker Enterprises," she began.

He gave a brief nod. "I'm the numbers guy."

"But never boring," she supplied.

"Don't get me started on cash-based versus accrual accounting," he said with dire warning.

"Definitely not something to get into on a first date. That is, unless she's a number cruncher herself." She added smoothly, "So what does a CFO do exactly?"

He frowned. "What sorts of dates are you planning to set me up with? I'm not going to have the patience to deal with a clueless beauty queen."

"Humor me."

He sighed. "I provide the financial strategy for

Whittaker Enterprises. We're a family-owned conglomerate with technology and real estate interests."

"I've read about you in the business section of the papers."

"Have you?" he murmured.

She got the impression he was intrigued by the fact, and wondered whether she'd revealed too much.

In Boston, the Whittakers and their family-run company were omnipresent. Over the years, she'd been unable to resist reading the articles about Matt. He'd remained single, playing the field, keeping mum about his private life, and at the same time, cutting a wide swath across the corporate landscape.

"Day to day," he went on, "I oversee the budget process and head up internal departments at Whittaker Enterprises, including administration and information technology."

"My eyes haven't glazed over yet."

His lips quirked up. "I romance numbers, and lust after a positive bottom line."

"Very funny."

"I get upset when figures don't balance, and nothing turns me on like a positive account."

"See?" she said encouragingly. "You *can* make this interesting."

"That's the day job. I moonlight investing in new companies."

She raised her brows. "You're a venture capitalist?"

"I'm an angel, sweetheart," he said, and the look he gave her was devilish.

Her mind tripped over his casual use of the endearment, even as she reminded herself *again* that their date wasn't *real*. Still, *this* Matthew Whittaker was a lot more seductive than the one she remembered from five years ago.

"I give seed money before venture capitalists get involved. We're called angels in the investment world."

"I see."

"The call I got earlier was about a company I'm thinking of investing in."

At her questioning look, he supplied, "The company founder is having trouble ceding control to professional management."

"Interesting."

He leaned forward, his eyes holding hers. "Tonight, though, all I'm interested in is investing in *you*."

As a come-on line, it was inventive and not half-bad.

After a moment, his eyes danced. "How'm I doing?"

"Not bad." She cleared her throat and tried to clear her mind. She really had to stay on topic. "We should discuss how you're going to describe yourself to a real date."

"Tell me more about the Fletcher Method," he countered.

"It's a little like detox. It's boot camp for entry into long-term commitment."

"By reprogramming men?"

"Both sides," she insisted. "It tries to clue in both parties about the expectations of the other side."

"In other words, remember Valentine's Day, her birthday and your anniversary."

"That's right, because, you know, there's nothing that says 'I love you' like a Valentine's Day card sent overnight express by your secretary."

He smiled. "Okay, I'll file that tip away. No more urgent deliveries arranged by the secretary."

"That's a start. Many men wake up well into their marriages scratching their heads and saying, 'What did I do wrong?' They don't have a clue as to why the woman is upset. I don't just want my clients to find a match, I want them to find a lasting match."

He contemplated her for a moment. "Matchmaking is a curious field for you to go into."

"You mean because I've had such bad luck in love myself?" She put into words what he'd left unstated.

He inclined his head.

"Not so curious. I have no intention of taking the plunge myself anytime soon."

"A bit cynical for a matchmaker, aren't you?"

"I suppose it's easy for you—or anyone—to think that, since I was stood up at the altar, but it's far from the truth."

The times any of her clients had bothered to delve into her past or had recognized her as Parker's jilted bride, she'd had the same answer at the ready. After all, no one wanted to take advice from a matchmaker who was unlucky in love.

In fact, the effects of a powerful cocktail of pain,

humiliation and, yes, seething anger had worn off long ago. These days, she was on an even keel—except when her past came back to visit her, especially in the form of an enigmatic corporate tycoon.

Matt looked at her quizzically. "Have you ever thought maybe *not* getting married to Parker was for the best?"

How many times had well-meaning friends and relatives said such stock phrases to her? *These things happen for a reason. It just wasn't meant to be. Time heals all wounds.*

"It was a little hard to remember why it may have been for the best when my credit card bill arrived," she said only half-jokingly.

She and Parker had divided the wedding costs, but it had been her wallet that had taken the relatively greater hit.

Matt raised his eyebrows. "Parker didn't offer to settle the bills because—"

"—because he ran out on me?" she finished for him, then shook her head.

"Most of the wedding vendors had to be paid ahead of time, and we split those costs," she admitted. "But, you know, since I decided to take the honeymoon trip anyway…"

"You got stuck with the cost."

She nodded. "Not the wisest move financially, but it proved to be brilliant spin and PR."

"Yes," he murmured, "I recall you caused a stir."

"I also insisted on repaying my parents for some

of the money they spent, since I felt it had been *my* mistake."

"Yours?"

She looked away from his penetrating gaze. "Yes, for maybe not seeing signs that things weren't perfect between me and Parker."

Parker's family had seemed cool and distant, but she'd attributed a lot of that to a general upper-class, old-money snootiness.

And then there'd been the *personal* signs. Under no circumstances, however, was she going to get into *that* with Matthew Whittaker.

He appeared satisfied with her answer, however. "But you sold the engagement ring to start Ideal Match."

"Yes, months later. Parker didn't bother asking for the ring back—" it was the one thing she could give Parker credit for, she admitted "—and frankly, I no longer knew where he was. I knew if I used the ring to pay off my debts, I'd never have a chance to get ahead."

She didn't bother mentioning the wedding gifts she'd had to return...the painful notes to guests...the parting with the wedding dress she couldn't bear to keep in her closet.

It had all been emotionally devastating, particularly since she'd always been a die-hard romantic. Growing up, her favorite game had been Here Comes the Bride. Her younger sister, Meghan, had played her maid of honor, and her younger brother,

Zach, had officiated, with one or another stuffed animal standing in for the groom.

Matt's expression was unreadable. "I have no idea where Parker is. Last I heard, traveling the world for business and pleasure." He paused. "Parker has a taste for chasing risky business ventures. I think he's hoping to return home in a blaze of glory."

That *did* sound like Parker, she admitted. When she'd met him at a late-night party, she'd reacted to his urbane charm and easy promises like a starry-eyed ingenue soaking up praise at her first audition.

What's more, she wasn't completely surprised that Matt and Parker didn't keep up. She knew Parker had asked Matt to be a groomsman more to strengthen a potentially important business relationship than anything else.

Aloud, she said, "In any case, I'm not single because I'm cynical or bitter. Otherwise, I'd never have stayed a matchmaker."

"What, then? Married to your job?"

She opened her mouth, then caught the teasing glimmer in his eyes.

"No, I'm simply not looking for anyone right now."

"And when you are?"

Why was he so curious? And why were they talking about this? "Then I'll know him when I see him."

She didn't add she was a fraud, and her Maybe Mr. Right would eventually discover that himself.

Until then she had a big test ahead of her, and that was finding Matt *his* Ms. Perfect. The sooner, the better.

Though she still had over two months before the *Sentinel* named its Most Eligible Bachelor again, her dealings with Matthew Whittaker were growing ever more complicated.

Fortunately, she knew just where to look for the perfect woman.

Lauren stared first at her computer screen, then out her office window, replaying the conversation of two days ago for the umpteenth time.

The truth was a bit more complicated than what she'd laid out for Matt. Sure, she had to socialize for work—scoping out available singles took a lot of time—but she'd always considered it a professional obligation.

She'd hit the Big 3-0 a couple of months ago, and she hadn't been in a steady relationship since getting stood up at the altar. Not only wasn't she looking for Mr. Right at the moment, she hadn't been looking for him in the past five years, either.

She'd ended up a statistic. And not one of those happy statistics, either. Not the kind that said I'm a happy, well-adjusted woman of the twenty-first century who is in control of her life. Instead, she'd already settled into a life of solitude with only Felix the feline for company.

After Parker, she'd gone through various stages of

breakup grief: shock and numbness, obsessive thinking and crying, and depression and despair. She'd resumed her life, but not as the same person. She was more aware and a lot more cautious these days.

The same caution was sounding a warning now. She'd caught herself thinking about Matt Whittaker not as a client, but as a *man*.

She sat back in her office chair. She'd tried to keep her professional demeanor intact the other night, but he'd confounded her, knocking her off balance.

Her eyes strayed back to her computer screen. She'd spent the better part of an hour scouring her database trying to come up with a list of potential dates for Matt.

Because she had to fight her attraction to him.

She'd learned some lessons from her experience with Parker, and the most important was that she was a failure in the bedroom as well as out.

Just then Candace breezed into her office, holding an arrangement of flowers. "These arrived. I'm dying to know who from!"

"For me?"

"Who else?" her receptionist said cheerily. "If they were for me, I'd already be pretending to have a headache and heading home early."

Lauren frowned. "But I haven't had a date recently."

"Tell me something I didn't already know." Candace set the flowers down at the corner of the desk. "Aren't they lovely?"

Lauren focused on the large bouquet of pink roses and lilies. "And expensive."

Candace folded her arms. "Maybe one of your clients got smart and realized the real catch is the matchmaker herself."

"Please." She and Candace had been down this road more times than she could count.

Candace plucked out the little white envelope tucked among the flowers and handed it to her. "Here. The world waits with bated breath."

Feigning disinterest, she sliced open the envelope and scanned the contents of the note inside.

Apologies for the cell phone lapse. Matt.

The words were scrawled in a masculine hand. As far as romance went, it was decidedly lacking.

Then she gave herself a mental shake. *Romance* and *Matt Whittaker* did not belong in the same sentence—at least where she was concerned.

"Well?" Candace asked.

"They're from Matt Whittaker."

"I knew it! Now there's a guy who's welcome to whisk me to Paris any day."

Her heart skipped a beat despite every rational thought to the contrary.

"You're jumping to conclusions." She got up and came around her desk to carry the flowers over to the side cabinet, where she could remove the clear plastic that surrounded them and add some more water. "He's just apologizing for being rude the other night."

"Oh." Some of the wind went out of Candace's sails as she followed her over to the side cabinet. "Still, sending flowers was a nice move, and, c'mon, the guy is pure beefcake underneath those conservative suits and power ties."

"I'm supposed to be hooking him up with a down-to-earth woman."

Candace held out her hands as if to say, voilà. "Have you told him about your humble origins?"

"Dad works for the school board, and Mom is a schoolteacher. Hardly fancy, but I wasn't running around barefoot, either." She didn't bother explaining *down-to-earth* for someone in Matt Whittaker's position meant a woman who was polite to the household help.

"Work with me."

"I am." She tossed the plastic wrap into a garbage bin. "I hired you after you struck out on the first nine interviews the employment agency sent you on, remember?"

Candace shrugged. "What can I say? My charms as a gum-chewing smart mouth are lost on some people. Go figure."

Lauren laughed despite herself. She'd hired Candace when she'd first started her business and couldn't afford to pay market rate even to a receptionist. Since then, the two of them had been through thick and thin together.

Candace watched as she fiddled with the flower arrangement. "I'll never understand why you haven't taken your pick from the men who've walked through the door here."

"You know why. We don't date the clients."

"Well, you don't."

She stopped and gave Candace an inquiring look.

Candace shrugged. "Only the continent-hopping scuba diver after he was a client here." Pause. "And, oh yeah, maybe the airline pilot with the hot—"

"I get the picture."

Candace shrugged. "Do you think I took this job because of the fantastic pay? A girl's got to fish at the nearest stream."

"Yes, but does it have to be off the company pier?"

Candace held up her hands as if to express, what can I say? "Let's get back to Matt Whittaker."

"Too starchy around the collar."

"But fat in the pocketbook," Candace countered.

"Have you no shame?"

"In a word? No."

"He was a groomsman at the infamous nonwedding."

Candace's eyes widened. "*Yours?*"

"Who else's?"

"Is he still in touch with Parker?"

"I don't think so, though Matt said, last he heard, Parker was traveling the world."

"You know, if I'd been your maid of honor, you

wouldn't have to wonder where Parker was. He'd have been chopped liver long before now."

Lauren rolled her eyes. "Yes, well, as you'll recall, *the two of us hadn't met yet.*"

Instead, her sister, Meghan, had been her maid of honor. The two of them had flown to Bora Bora, dined on mahimahi, sipped kava drinks and danced under the stars.

Candace shrugged, as if the fact the two of them hadn't known each other back then was beside the point. "So, are you going to hold it against him?"

She didn't have to ask what Candace meant. Yet, it wasn't just that Matt had remained impassive on the day that would live on in infamy to Lauren.

"Well?" Candace asked.

"Our relationship was always…awkward." She stared down at the flowers she was fiddling with before dropping her hands. "There's always been a sort of quiet intensity in his eyes."

"Oh…wow." Candace sighed—a dreamy look crossing her face—then snapped back to attention. "And that's a bad thing? Honey, if he'd fixed me with those magnetic blues of his, I'd have been the one doing the jilting at the altar."

Lauren wondered why she was standing here talking about Matt. He was her past, and the only way he was useful to her now was as a cash cow for Ideal Match.

"Don't you have some work to do?" she asked pointedly.

Candace cracked a smile, then handed her a piece of paper. "Heartbreak Phil left two messages."

"Only two?"

Heartbreak Phil was their name for a client who was all smiles, but had axed more dates than she could count.

"He had a flight to Phoenix to catch, so his day was cut short," Candace said. "The first phone message was about his date last night, the second at our backup number was to make sure you'd gotten the first."

"Naturally."

Candace grinned. "Wonder how he's broken up with her this time."

Lauren grimaced. "I don't want to know."

At first, Heartbreak Phil had tried to insist it was her responsibility as his matchmaker to do the breaking up for him.

"That's why I hired you," he'd said.

She'd finally convinced him that breaking things off was a social skill he needed to master.

Unfortunately, Heartbreak Phil had implemented her advice in unexpected ways, such as delivering a "Dear Jane" letter by e-mail—with a confirmation copy by overnight courier for good measure.

The phone rang, and Candace strode over to Lauren's desk. "Let's hope it's not Heartbreak Phil for round three," she said over her shoulder, before picking up the receiver.

"Feeling lonely? Feeling blue? Have we got a

match for you!" Candace went on more sedately, "Ideal Match. What can we do for you?"

Lauren rolled her eyes. She'd tried to get Candace to drop the ridiculous theme song, but most of her clients seemed amused by it.

Candace laughed at something the caller said, then pressed the hold button and gave the receiver to her before taking a step toward the door. "Our favorite CFO holding for Dr. Date."

Four

"Thank you for the flowers. They just arrived, and they're lovely."

Matt tried to read Lauren's voice as he paced in his Atlanta hotel room. This business trip had been one difficult meeting after another, and he was ready to head home.

Loosening his tie with one hand, he said, "You're welcome. My secretary didn't arrange to send them. I wanted you to know your tutoring isn't going to waste."

"What a relief."

"So have you come up with some matches yet?"

In reality, it was the last thought on his mind. He'd called her because he'd had a moment...

because he'd wanted to know if she'd gotten his bouquet…and because, frankly, he'd wanted to talk to her—judge her reaction.

He hadn't been able to put her out of his mind since their dinner together a couple of days ago. He'd told himself it was only because he'd been giving some thought to this whole matchmaking business.

She cleared her throat. "Yes. Yes, I have some wonderful matches."

"Great."

He heard some clicking noises in the background and assumed she was searching for the right documents on her computer.

"I have a fabulous client named Melanie," she said, her voice all business. "She's a model and actress—"

"No actresses."

"Why not?"

"Hollywood types are too self-involved."

"But Melanie is a *classically trained* actress," Lauren argued. "She does theater. Her mother is on the board of directors of Massachusetts Youth Theater."

"Too artsy for me."

It all sounded great on paper, but somehow as Lauren described a woman he'd never even met, he found he couldn't work up any enthusiasm.

There was a pause on the line before Lauren said, "Okay, moving right along. Valerie is a wonderful woman who also happens to be a management consultant at Bain & Co."

"No way." Here he was on more familiar territory, and he had no trouble cutting her off.

"What? Why?" Lauren sounded startled. "Valerie's a career go-getter, but she also loves sports and the outdoors. She happens to be a big hockey fan, and I know you played in college."

"Great," he responded, "because the only time we'll be able to catch a game is on TV at the airport. Management consultants do some serious traveling. We'll never even be able to schedule a date."

"Okaaay." Lauren's tone moved from reasonable to crisp. "Next we have Bethany—"

He came to a halt. "Bethany Collingsworth?"

"Yes. How did you guess?"

"How many women named Bethany do you know?" he asked mockingly. "So, is she a paying client, or just someone you're acquainted with?"

"Why are you interested?" she countered.

"I'm not, but I'll take it from your evasive answer she's a paying client."

"What's wrong with her?"

"She's looking for a rich husband."

"But she's a trust fund baby," she retorted skeptically.

"And said trust fund is about to see its limit."

"What?" Lauren's voice sounded exasperated over the telephone. "How do you know that?"

"I never reveal my sources."

Boston's upper echelons constituted a small world, and even he'd heard about Bethany "What

Are You Worth?" Collingsworth, not the least because of her unsuccessful attempt to land his brother Noah not too long before his marriage.

Lauren sighed. "You're going to have to give me some time to come up with more names."

He could tell from her tone of voice that she felt like throttling him, and he fought a smile. "Take heart, sweetness. Everyone has to deal with the fact that the client is always right, including me."

"Easy for you to say," she replied. "You're the client in this situation."

A laugh escaped him. "Lucky me."

"I'm going to give the speech I usually give here about staying flexible and keeping an open mind."

"Another lesson?" he mocked. "When do we start?"

"Not this weekend. I'm busy."

He felt an unwelcome stab of jealousy. Was she seeing someone? She'd said she wasn't looking for anyone right now, but she could have a date from time to time.

"Business or pleasure?" he asked casually.

He could sense her hesitation before she said, "A little of both."

"The mystery deepens," he said probingly.

She sighed. "Well, if you must know, I volunteer at a retirement community."

"As a matchmaker?" he asked in surprise.

"Love is for the young at heart."

"Apparently."

"Now who's being cynical?" she said. "Actually, I'm attending the wedding of a couple I introduced. The groom is seventy-seven, and the bride is seventy-five. They're both widowed, and they're having a party for some friends and family."

Something in the tone of her voice—a hint of vulnerability?—made him soften. "When's the big occasion?"

"Late Sunday afternoon."

He knew what he was going to say next, though he realized it wasn't his wisest move. "Do you have a date?"

She gave a dismissive laugh. "Yes, my car, which is taking me there."

"Trade up." He kept his tone casual. "I know a macho Lexus SUV that's looking for a good time."

"I—"

"Consider it part of the job of reforming me," he said before she could decline. "Otherwise, I'd be working."

There was a pause. "Well…I suppose it would do you some good to see an example of true love in action."

He felt the release of tension he hadn't known he'd been holding. "When do I pick you up?"

It was déjà vu, Lauren thought.

The last time she'd been in a church with Matthew Whittaker, she'd been dressed in ivory satin, ready to marry another man.

When she'd agreed to have Matt accompany her today, she hadn't been thinking about how it would conjure up feelings that had lain dormant for years. She'd been thinking only about exposing Matt to romance in its purest form.

Purely for the sake of improving his attractiveness to women, she told herself. *Herself excluded.*

She stole a look at him now, sitting beside her in the pew of the small chapel that served the Pine Hill retirement community. He looked austere yet heart-stoppingly handsome in a charcoal-gray pinstripe suit and pale blue-and-yellow tie.

Her pulse jumped.

She'd been nervous all day, waiting for the moment when Matt would arrive to pick her up in his car, trying to decide what to wear.

She'd eventually selected a powder-blue, midcalf-length chiffon dress with sheer sleeves and a sheer overlay on the bodice. It was one of her favorite outfits because of its unabashed nod to fantasy, and she'd worn it to a trio of weddings already.

Still, she'd been skittish when she'd greeted Matt—that is, until she'd seen the look of pure hunger in his eyes before he'd banked it.

Matt stopped looking around and leaned toward her. "I'm impressed. This place is like a small village. Who was the developer?"

She named a small firm in the Boston area.

Matt nodded. "Whittaker Enterprises needs to get into the retirement community construction market."

She wasn't sure whether he was kidding or not, but she had to agree Pine Hill was an attractive place. Residents could choose from a variety of living arrangements, from small cottages to an apartment complex to an assisted-living center. The full range of amenities was provided and then some, from dog walking to lawn management to housekeeping. The recreational center hosted dances, parties, exercise classes and more.

Her own involvement had started in a roundabout way, after an older client, a widower in his fifties, had told her about his mother, a Pine Hill resident, who wished her community had a matchmaker.

She'd contacted the Pine Hill administrative office and was assigned a small space, where people could come in to meet her on weekends and tell her what they were looking for.

In the wake of the Parker Disaster—as she'd taken to calling the jilting—it had beaten sitting at home, watching a chick flick on TV and weeping into a bowl of popcorn.

Her role, though, had mushroomed from part-time volunteer to much more. She'd gotten to know and develop a soft spot for some of the residents—from Agnes who refused to date a man with a toupee, to Floyd and his collection of toy soldiers and battle reenactments.

She became a sort of part-time recreational director in her quest to get to know the residents and figure out who to match with whom.

Looking at Matt now, she wondered what he thought of it all, and realized with a jolt he was the first man who'd accompanied her to Pine Hill.

Just then, the music changed, alerting the assembled guests, some fifty in all, that the processional was about to begin.

She and Matt rose and turned along with the other guests to look at the back of the chapel.

As the bride, dressed in a simple gray suit, entered to the notes of Purcell's "Trumpet Tune," Lauren felt her eyes mist.

She blinked rapidly, hoping Matt didn't notice. It would be horrifying if he knew what a closet romantic she was—*still was.*

She watched as the bride reached the groom and they joined hands before turning to face the officiant.

"Dear Friends," the minister began, "we are gathered here today to join Veronica and Albert in matrimony...."

Beside her, Matt faced straight ahead, his expression inscrutable.

She sat, waiting for her turn, waiting to be called to say her piece for these two people she'd helped bring together.

Her own marriage had been stillborn, and she always found it cathartic to witness a wedding go off without a hitch.

When her turn came, she went up to the lectern and, her eyes straying to Matt's, she quoted from memory Sir Edwin Arnold's poem "Somewhere" about two lonely souls meeting and blending into a perfect whole.

When she got to the words *perfect whole,* she felt Matt's eyes on her like a steady heat. A cleansing feeling washed over her, as if layers of concealment were falling away from both of them, and they were seeing each other *as they were.*

The spell broke only when a musician struck a chord, signaling the start of the next part of the program.

As she walked back to her seat, she didn't look at Matt, not trusting herself with her surfacing emotions.

She looked straight ahead through the wafting strands of "Ave Maria" and up to the part of the ceremony when the vows were to be exchanged.

As the bride began with the words "I, Veronica, take you, Albert," Lauren felt the tears begin to well.

She blinked to hold them at bay.

"…to have and to hold from this day forward, for better or for worse…"

A tear escaped and trailed down her cheek. Then another.

"…to love and to cherish from this day forward until death do us part."

Suddenly she felt Matt's warm grip, engulfing her hand in his own. Surprised, she glanced at him, but he sat facing forward, his jaw set.

By the time the minister uttered the words "You may kiss the bride," she'd become a leaky mess.

Matt glanced at her, and she turned to look back at him. Let him think what he wanted, she thought. She couldn't hide the evidence of how much the ceremony had moved her, and there was no use trying.

But instead of sardonic amusement, or impassive lack of comprehension, she was greeted with eyes that were serious and intent.

Her mind turned to mush as he leaned in and kissed away one tear, then another.

"No tissues," he murmured as he sat back and faced front again.

Dumbfounded, she stared at his profile for a moment before turning to look at the now-beaming bride and groom.

As she joined the rest of the congregation in applause, she wondered at Matt's reaction. He'd reached for her hand and kissed her tears away.

Perhaps he was learning something about romance.

But was he simply showing her he was listening to her, or did his actions mean something more?

It was so confusing, and the last thing she needed, she reminded herself, was for her relationship with Matthew Whittaker to become more of a tangle.

He needed to learn how to think more with his heart than with his head, but she had the opposite problem, and this time she wasn't going to let anything get in the way of what made logical sense: getting Matthew Whittaker married off and sealing her reputation as Boston's premier matchmaker.

As they departed the chapel and made their way to the reception at a nearby restaurant, she caught the speculative looks of other guests, most of them residents of Pine Hill.

Belatedly, she realized just how much conjecture she'd provoked by bringing Matthew Whittaker as her date to the wedding.

In fact, once they reached the restaurant, it didn't take long for the comments to flow like beer at a college party.

As one well-meaning lady said, glancing flirtatiously at Matt, "I'd marry him myself if I were twenty years younger and one husband short."

Never mind, Lauren thought drolly, that twenty years would still leave her at least a full decade older than Matt.

Still, *that* comment was not as mortifying as those that followed. The residents of Pine Hill had a field day dissecting her social life.

"Sweetie," one of the resident doyennes said, within earshot of Matt, "he looks like he'd be great in bed."

She felt herself burning up with embarrassment, and the only thing that stopped her from dissolving into a pile of ash was the fact that Matt was engrossed in a conversation with a retired construction company owner.

She didn't want to think about the extent of Matthew Whittaker's prowess as a lover. She didn't want a reminder of how much she came up short in that department.

She almost breathed a sigh of relief when she found herself on the small dance floor with Matt.

He was a good dancer. Their height difference didn't even register as he guided her across the dance floor with the subtle pressure of his hand at her back.

He smelled of soap—some clean, fresh scent undoubtedly targeted to men—and his skin looked smooth, newly shaven and inviting to the touch. She itched to run her hand along his jaw.

She purposely looked away and tried to focus on the fact that her mission tonight was to expose Matt to romance in all its flavors. She couldn't have him talking numbers with all his dates, after all.

"I like your friends," he said, drawing her attention back to him. "They're a tight-knit bunch."

"You don't know the half of it," she muttered, thinking of the personal comments she'd been getting all evening.

"What?" He searched her face.

"They like you."

The corner of his mouth lifted. "Haven't you heard? I'm supposed to be great in bed."

Her face flamed. "Er—"

"What I want to know," he said, his lips twitching, "is why I should be learning all this dating etiquette when my skills as a lover are speaking for themselves."

The word *lover* caused her nerve endings to riot. Since there was no safe response to his comment, she said lightly, "You can fox-trot and waltz with the best of them twice your age."

His eyes twinkled, as if he saw right through her attempt to change topics.

"When we were little," he said finally, "my mother enrolled us in dance class."

"You're joking." She had a passing acquaintance with all the Whittakers, and she couldn't imagine Matt and his brothers, macho guys all, practicing the box step.

"It was a monumental effort getting me and my brothers to behave." He grinned. "My brother Noah decided to engage in guerilla tactics by sabotaging himself, tripping over feet and hoping to get booted out of class."

"And did it work?"

"No." He laughed. "But he earned himself a trip to the pediatrician when my mother worried he was having trouble with his balance. That, and he got a reputation as the class clown."

"I loved dance class."

He eyed her. "I bet you were one of those girls who wanted to be a ballerina when she grew up."

"From the first to the fourth grades," she said wistfully. "I only wish my legs had grown longer."

He leaned to the side, pretending to examine her, then his eyes met hers again. "There's nothing wrong with them, as far as I can tell."

The air between them crackled.

"Thank you, but I was like those girls whose feet you and your brothers were stepping on."

He gave her a fixed look. "I doubt I'd have tripped

over your feet," he said in a low voice. "I may have tried other things to get your attention, but not that."

After a moment, she was the one to finally look away.

This close, she could feel the heat emanating from his hard body. Her breasts tingled in response. *Everything tingled.*

It had been a mistake to have him accompany her today. It had taken five years, but her life was nice and well ordered now—just the way she wanted it. She was unprepared and unwilling to open the door to emotions from her past.

She needed to find him an appropriate woman and fast, so he could make a clean exit from her life. Everything else was too messy to contemplate.

She promised herself that, as soon as she got back to her office, she'd reapply herself with zeal to the task of finding Matt potential dates. And she refused to dwell on why that thought was depressing.

Unfortunately, Matt seemed unwilling to cooperate with the plan she'd just concocted in her mind.

He chatted with the other guests, made them laugh and, in response to probing questions, did nothing to dispel the impression he was more than her client.

In short, he was a hit with the Pine Hill crowd, and she was left to wonder at this side of Matthew Whittaker—a side that was charming and polished and easy to talk to, and emphatically *not* on display five years ago.

At the end of the evening, as they chatted pleasantly with the newlyweds before saying their goodbyes, Matt slid an arm around her waist.

"We can't recommend Lauren enough to you," Veronica said. "I'd never have met Albert otherwise. After his first wife died, he left his house only to play golf and visit his grandchildren."

"I'm glad Lauren invited me along today," Matt said. "It was a beautiful wedding."

"You should try getting married yourself," Albert countered.

"I intend to." Matt winked. "In the meantime, I'm getting polished."

Before Lauren could react, Matt leaned down and brushed her lips with his own.

Five

Three weeks later, as Lauren restlessly waited in her office for Matt to arrive, she relived *the kiss* even as she knew their showdown this evening was overdue.

This wasn't the first time, of course, she'd replayed *the kiss* in her mind. But she told herself it happened when she was in bed at night, and at odd moments when she let her mind wander.

The kiss had been the merest brush of lips, but its effect had stayed with her. His lips had felt warm, smooth and tempting.

Of course, for the Pine Hill residents who had witnessed it, *the kiss* had been the last proof they needed that she and Matt were heading to the altar.

For her part, she'd been forced to acknowledge her attraction, however inadvisable. But she'd told herself any woman would find Matt attractive. *He was attractive.*

At the same time, since they'd attended the wedding together, she'd been running possible candidates by Matt with a vengeance. She was determined to find him a wife—the type of woman she thought he was looking for.

Each time she set up a date for him, though, she felt depressed imagining him wining and dining—not to mention, *kissing*—another woman. On those nights, she kept herself busy, even if it meant scrubbing the bathroom, in order to avoid going crazy over thoughts of him with another woman.

It was a classic case of cognitive dissonance—pursuing two contradictory goals at once. Her body clamored to jump into bed with Matt, but her mind refused to let her repeat the mistakes of the past. She was both trying to set him up with another woman ASAP and giving in to an inexcusable flirtation herself.

And getting romantically involved with Matthew Whittaker *would* be a mistake. Matt came from the same world as her ex-fiancé. He was cerebral whereas she was all heart. If she got involved with him, not only could she say goodbye to Ideal Match's potentially biggest success story to date, but her heart would be mashed in the process. She wasn't in his league in any respect.

Lauren sighed. She shouldn't be giving advice to other people, she needed it herself.

On top of it all, Matt had become her most frustrating and intractable client, even besting Heartbreak Phil. He'd found fault with every single woman she'd set him up with. It wasn't that she expected him to find Ms. Right immediately—though the clock was ticking on the naming of the *Sentinel*'s new Most Eligible Bachelor—but that none of his matches progressed beyond a cursory first date.

Thus, today's powwow.

As if on cue, she heard a door open and close in the reception room, followed by Candace's called-out greeting to Matt.

Lauren reached the door to her office in time to see Candace, already with her coat on, heading toward the office's outer door.

Catching Candace's wink, she frowned.

Her receptionist seemed all too eager to leave her alone with Matt. And because six o'clock was Candace's usual departure time, she couldn't argue, especially since Candace had claimed—only half-convincingly despite a practiced and unwavering gaze—that she had agreed to babysit her neighbor's kids again.

"See you tomorrow!" Candace called.

When the office's door clicked shut, her eyes went to Matt. She was alone in the big, silent reception room with her newly minted Mr. Impossible, a name she'd coined for him last night…while in bed…when she'd again been thinking about him when she shouldn't.

He'd discarded his coat on a nearby chair and was standing in the middle of the room with his hands shoved in his suit pockets.

In order to accommodate his schedule, she'd agreed to meet after the end of the business day. And the truth was this meeting had been put off long enough. He was driving her crazy, rejecting every candidate she'd sent his way.

They'd talked a bit by phone after some of his dates—when she'd been careful to avoid all mention of his behavior at Veronica and Albert's wedding—but she'd gotten pat answers from him.

Still, even as he seemed to fill up all the available space in her office, she steeled herself for the discussion ahead, because she knew it was imperative he change his attitude.

"You're sabotaging your chances of meeting the right woman," she said without preamble.

"And hello to you, too," he said with lazy amusement.

She felt the telltale tingling along her nerve endings and charged ahead to avoid thinking about how much he made her conscious of being a woman.

"Don't try to sidestep the discussion."

"I'm not sidestepping anything," he said in a mild voice.

She folded her arms. "You told Monica that if she wanted to catch a husband, she'd be better off enrolling in a degree program instead of majoring at Salon U. to keep her hair a precise shade of champagne blond."

He arched a brow. "You disagree?"

She threw up her hands. "She's an heiress. She can afford it."

"Obviously not, if she needed to hire you. There's usually no shortage of guys who'd be happy to marry an heiress."

"Not you, however."

"I don't need the money."

He looked calm and unperturbed, and at the same time, radiated sex appeal. The observation riled her even more.

"In any case," he said, "I believe my requirements included being down-to-earth. How does Monica qualify?"

"Down-to-earth socialites are a bit thin on the ground," she replied tartly.

"You know, I don't recollect listing *socialite* among my requirements."

Of course, she thought, *that* requirement went without saying. His type wanted to marry *well*, and not to some nobody from Sacramento with school-teacher parents who were strictly middle-class.

"You said you were looking for someone with the acumen for business entertainment," she countered.

"*Business* being the operative word there."

"What about Sarah then? Her father was a surgeon, but she's as down-to-earth as you can get.

She started a handmade soaps business. She should have suited the entrepreneurial side of you."

"Too back-to-nature." He shrugged. "Besides, there was no chemistry. We talked shop all night."

"How about Lily? What was wrong with her?"

He arched a brow. "Save me from fashionistas."

"Amanda?"

"She was a public relations executive. I got the impression she was less interested in me than in a job as a spokesperson at Whittaker Enterprises."

She folded her arms. "What about Peyton?"

"Advertising. She took one look at me and saw a potential client."

"Pamela?" She'd been sure she had a hit there. "She's a TV anchor, and she's as polished as they come."

"Too interested in herself."

She bit back a sigh of exasperation.

He contemplated her for a second. "You've tried to set me up with umpteen candidates and failed. You know there's only one thing left for you to do, don't you?"

"And that would be?" she asked coolly, dropping her arms.

"Date me yourself."

Caught off guard, she retorted, "Don't be absurd."

He sized her up. "Why? What's wrong with you?"

"It appears you've misunderstood the nature of the services we offer in this office," she said, her words coated with frost. "I'm in the business of finding you a lifetime partner, not providing you with a fling."

"Who said anything about a fling? I'm talking about mutual enjoyment."

"You want sexual services in exchange for my fee."

"No," he drawled, "just suggesting we see where things lead."

She knew where things would lead, and she didn't have to sleep with him to find out. She was incapable of satisfying him, but was determined he never know. Her heart was retired, and her sexual prowess nonexistent.

She affected an expression of cool disdain. "Well, that's an approach I haven't heard before. Just come out and ask for sex."

"You're deliberately misunderstanding me. I'm suggesting we explore the attraction simmering between us."

"Maybe on your part, but I don't know what you mean."

"Liar," he said softly. "Don't you think we should talk about that kiss?"

"I'm your matchmaker." They were *not* having this conversation.

"And isn't your job to know if my sexual technique is lacking?" he asked, sauntering closer.

"I'm sorry," she said repressively, "but my services don't go beyond general advice in that department."

"I recall signing up for the total package—the works."

As he came closer, she took an involuntary step back, then another.

The glittering intent in his eyes spoke of want... need...desire.

"Keep moving, sweetness."

"This is ridiculous," she said, her voice carrying a note of breathlessness. "You can't chase me around my office."

"Really? Isn't that what I'm doing?"

He trapped her against the reception desk, and she leaned back, perched on the smooth mahogany edge.

He set his hands down on either side of her, bracing himself on his arms.

Her heart beat faster. "This is ridiculous."

"You already said that," he murmured.

This close, he was overpowering. She felt as if she were drowning in his blue eyes. Then her gaze dropped to his mouth, and she thought of that mouth on hers and shuddered.

He leaned forward, his legs brushing against hers and she felt the hard, unyielding muscle beneath the veneer of civility lent by his business suit.

"What's the matter?" he said. "Finding it hard to deny the attraction?"

"No," she snapped, because he'd hit too close to the truth. "Just prepared to prove how wrong you are."

His eyes glinted as he took up the challenge. "I guess you're ready to put it to the test."

As he leaned in, his eyes held hers before lowering, zeroing in on her mouth as she did on his.

When his lips touched hers, the kiss was all heat, and she was surrounded by the male scent that clung to him.

His lips moved over hers, plumping her lips, then soothing and smoothing, drawing a reaction from her.

The feel of him was intoxicating. She raised her hands to place them on his chest and gave a nip at his lips.

His response was swift as he took the kiss deeper.

Their mouths clung, the kiss long and searching, and his hands came up to caress her back and mold her to him.

And she went—*willingly.*

She was swamped by sensation. Her breasts, pressed against his chest, felt tight and sensitive. Warmth spread low in her abdomen and settled at the juncture of her legs.

Dimly, she wondered at his effect on her. He was a glorified accountant and Parker's would-be groomsman. He couldn't be having this effect on her.

But he was.

Gradually, he brought them up from the depths, drawing back until he was feathering light kisses on her lips.

His lips wandered from her mouth to her jaw and to the soft spot behind her ear, then traveled downward.

Bending her backward, he leaned in to kiss the hollow of her throat. She clung to his shoulders, her leg rubbing against him, the need to be closer to him overwhelming.

His hand began to work at the buttons of her blouse to give them what they both wanted.

"Oops, sorry!"

Lauren jumped and broke away from Matt.

Glancing over, she discovered Candace standing inside the office's front door.

Lauren wasn't sure who was more surprised or embarrassed. Actually, she amended after a beat, Candace looked more intrigued then anything.

She, on the other hand, was mortified. She sat perched on the edge of her desk, one leg wedged between Matt's, and the other bent, his hand grasping her thigh where her skirt had ridden up. Her white blouse gaped open, revealing her lacy, beige-colored bra, and her lips still felt puffy from his kisses.

She stole a look at him. He managed to look cool and unflappable even with mussed hair and a visible arousal—though only she had evidence of the latter from the bulge resting against her thigh.

Candace spoke first. "Don't mind me. I just came back to look for an umbrella." When they all remained immobile, she added, "It's raining out."

Lauren placed her hands on Matt's chest and pushed, but when he took a step back, she knew it was only because he wanted to. Still, she took the opportunity to hop off her desk and fumble with the buttons of her blouse, attempting to restore some order to her clothes.

"Here, let me help." Matt's voice—deep and amused—sounded beside her.

She glared at him. She'd worked hard to cultivate a certain professional image, and now it was going up in a puff of smoke, even if it was just Candace who'd stumbled upon them.

More important, the stolen moment of passion was going to cost her dearly in terms of her own self-respect.

"Oh, look! Found it!" Candace made a show of spotting and grabbing a small umbrella that was lying on a mahogany file cabinet. Then grinning, she backed out of the room, pulling the office door shut as she went. "Don't stop on my account."

When the door clicked shut, the room was silent again.

She continued to concentrate on fixing her disheveled appearance.

"If she'd given us another minute," Matt said finally, "we'd have been tangled up together on the rug."

"That was a mistake," she managed.

"One that bears repeating."

"No," she said flatly, looking up at him.

Matt, the passionate lover of moments ago was gone, replaced by a cool observer who revealed nothing of his thoughts.

"No," she said more firmly. "That should never have happened."

"You blame me." He said it without inflection.

She shook her head. "I'm not going to take the easy way out. We were both willing participants."

"So you admit you enjoyed it." This time there was a note of satisfaction in his voice.

She waved her hand. "Whether I did or not doesn't matter. I'm not on the menu."

His brows came together. "That's a cop-out. What are you afraid of?"

"Nothing!" *Fear* had nothing to do with it, practicality did.

Still, he was hitting close to home, so she rushed to shift the conversation. "Why are we talking about me? The real issue here is you and the way you're acting."

His jaw hardened. He looked as if he wanted to continue arguing with her but thought better of it.

"If I need pointers," he said, his eyes glittering, "you'll just have to give me some more lessons."

Matt felt a jolt of lust.

Lauren was dressed in fitting colors for a Valentine's Day dinner, and he appreciated the results.

His gaze focused of its own volition at the V of Lauren's crushed velvet crimson top, which outlined her breasts to perfection. The top was the showcase above a long, pencil-straight skirt and black suede pumps.

She was studying the menu in the flickering candlelight, and he was taking the opportunity to study her.

He'd been on his best behavior since the confrontation in her office last week, but he could sense she still considered his motives suspect.

He'd been able to pull some strings to get a last-minute dinner reservation at Aujourd'hui, in the Four Seasons Hotel. It was one of Boston's top restaurants, and its decadent ambience, overlooking the Public Garden, was suited to a romantic tryst, just the way he wanted it.

It had taken some maneuvering to get Lauren to reserve Valentine's Day for him and his next lesson in dating etiquette, and he wasn't about to blow the opportunity.

He'd convinced her to make their next lesson for Valentine's Day by arguing there was no reason they shouldn't. If her goal was to awaken his romantic instincts, there was no better day for it. They both had the night free, and his schedule was otherwise packed—okay, maybe not *that* packed, he admitted to himself now. Still, she'd been doubtful, but he'd dangled the irresistible lure of marrying him off.

So now he had her just where he wanted her.

Ever since the wedding at Pine Hill, he'd been on a rapid slide to lust…passion…desire. Lauren's vulnerable side had been on rare display that day, and he'd been intrigued and attracted.

He'd thought about her, and only her, while on those ridiculous dates she'd arranged for him, and soon he'd found himself making up reasons to reject one candidate after another.

Except the reasons weren't made up. His little matchmaker was doomed to failure, because there was only one woman he wanted, and she was sitting across from him, dressed in a crushed velvet crimson top.

Whether Lauren knew it or not, tonight was the start of his plan to seduce her, and he planned to make the most of it, though he didn't want to come on *too* strong and scare her off.

Now, after they ordered, he took the hand Lauren had resting on the table and drew it toward him.

He gazed into her eyes, his thumb drawing lazy circles on her inner wrist.

"Did I make a good choice?" he murmured.

"Hmm?" she asked, appearing distracted by the motion of his hand.

He nodded around them. "The restaurant. I'm hoping you like it."

"Yes. Er—of course." She looked down at their hands.

"I'm practicing," he said in reply to her unspoken question.

She looked up, uncomprehendingly, and he forced himself to keep a straight face.

"Practicing for a date," he explained.

He planned to exploit the blurred line between *practice* and *reality* to his advantage in his quest to have her.

"Oh."

He could feel her rapid pulse. "Because I just want to be sure I'm getting it right."

She wet her lips, and he almost groaned aloud in response.

"Ah…yes."

"How'm I doing?" he murmured, striving to keep his face innocent when all he wanted to do was hoist her across the table and devour her.

A little line appeared between her brows. "What?"

He nodded at their joined hands. "How am I doing with my practice routine?"

"Oh, right."

He bit the inside of his cheek to keep from smiling.

"Well…" She cleared her throat. "Umm, you don't want to come on too strong, but you do want to let her know you're interested."

"Like this?" he said in a low voice, raising her hand to his lips, his eyes never leaving hers.

Her eyes widened. "Yes, ah, just like that. You'll also want to compliment her."

He lowered her hand and laced his fingers through hers. "Back in college, what qualified as a compliment was a bad pickup line."

"Such as?" she asked curiously, relaxing a fraction.

"You don't want to know."

"I've heard it all before," she insisted. "Besides, whatever you say, just make sure you personalize it for her."

"All right." He leaned in and said with exaggerated seductiveness, "I must be lost at sea, because, baby, I'm drowning in your big blue-green eyes."

Her laugh sounded breathless. "You're right. That *is* terrible."

"You've got a killer body, because, honey, it's slaying me."

"Stop," she pleaded.

They were joking, but a strong undercurrent of sexual awareness ran through the conversation.

She sat back, and he finally let her slip her hand from his, breaking the spell.

"Bad pickup lines aside," she said, "good communication is the key to a healthy relationship."

He wondered what she'd say if he communicated what he *really* wanted from her.

When he'd walked into Ideal Match for the first time, his intention had been to deal with a nagging problem in the same swift and efficient way as he dealt with everything in his life.

Yes, his visit had been tinged with more than a little curiosity about Lauren herself, but he'd thought only about putting to rest any lingering feelings— of guilt or otherwise—by handing Lauren her juiciest client to date, namely, *him* in his incarnation as Boston's number one bachelor for two years running.

Now he thought maybe he'd been deluding himself. Maybe he'd always been deluding himself.

He remembered the sucker punch to the stomach—the way he'd felt as if the wind had been knocked out of him—when during some long-ago society function, Parker had introduced Lauren to him as his fiancée. He'd quickly quelled the feeling, not wanting to examine it too closely.

Parker, he told himself now, was in the distant past and no longer even on the landscape. At some point, he should tell Lauren about events the night before she was to marry Parker—but he'd pick the time and place.

If he had a shot with Lauren at the moment, there was no reason why he shouldn't take it.

"What should we talk about then?" he found himself saying.

"You should ask her about her interests."

"Okay, tell me about your volunteer work." He was interested in knowing everything about her.

She seemed to relax a little more. "The auction for the Boston Operatic League is coming up this weekend."

He searched his brain. "The one where you were still looking for male volunteers to model the designer clothing?"

She gave him an innocent smile. "That's right."

He read her expression and sighed inwardly.

He'd just found what he'd been searching for— a way to score points with Lauren. The problem was he might become a laughingstock as a result.

Still, he wanted Lauren in his bed, and he'd be willing to wear flamingo pink if that's what it took to get her there.

"So," he said, resigned to his fate, "what'll I be wearing? Sean John, or Joseph Abboud?"

Six

There were some things Lauren never thought she'd see in her life. Matthew Whittaker parading down a catwalk was one of them.

She took in the admiring female looks Matt was attracting as he came down the runway again—this time in, yes, a Sean John suit—and stomped down the jealous sparks those looks aroused.

Candace was right. Matt was pure beefcake. He was the embodiment of masculine sex appeal, but it was a subliminal message from underneath all that designer clothing.

Still, it was a message obviously received by the women at this afternoon's event in the auditorium of the Boston Operatic League. Some were whispering to their friends, while others were throwing Matt looks of such open invitation she felt like jumping onto the catwalk herself and running interference.

And *that* was crazy. After all, she'd spent the past several weeks trying to achieve exactly *this*—getting Matt hooked up with a suitable woman. She'd first suggested participating today to Matt as a way for him to attract the right type of woman by promoting himself as someone who supported the arts.

Other organizers had recruited their husbands, fiancés or boyfriends to model in today's show, but Matt was the only unattached bachelor participating, and the fact that one of Boston's most desirable and wealthiest bachelors was strutting his substantial assets hadn't been lost on the reporters in the audience.

Journalists from the *Boston Sentinel, The Boston Globe* and the *Boston Herald,* as well as smaller papers and magazines, were out in force and gobbling up this story like kids at a candy-dispensing machine.

She could see tomorrow's news stories. Still, it was too late to put the genie back in the bottle.

Of course, Matt wasn't helping matters. Every time he came down the runway, he looked straight at her, his gaze unwavering—hot, hard and full of promise.

She wondered how a man with the looks of a *GQ* model, the body of an athlete, and the gaze of a stripper could hide out under the guise of a dried-out corporate titan. She'd seen no glimpse of the man underneath five years ago. But now he heated her blood and sent her pulse racing.

She'd barely survived Valentine's Day and their "practice" dinner date. The candlelight, wine and romantic ambiance, combined with Matt's lambent gaze, had been a heady mix.

Only when Matt turned away to walk back up the makeshift runway was the spell between them broken.

Breathing more easily, Lauren scanned the audience and belatedly noticed the Whittakers sitting in the last row.

The Whittakers were staples on Boston's society scene and charity circuit, known for their generous giving as well as their fabulous looks and in the case of the women, their fashion sense.

Matt's oldest brother, Quentin, CEO of Whittaker Enterprises, was there with his wife, Elizabeth, an interior designer. Quentin was tall and dark haired, rivaling Matt in his taste for conservative suits, while his wife was curvaceous, auburn haired and striking. Lauren knew from the newspapers, and the occasions when she'd run into the Whittakers at one function or another, that Elizabeth and Quentin were parents to a little boy.

Quentin sat next to Matt's younger brother, Noah, a VP at the family company and a former professional race car driver. He'd come with his wife, Kayla, herself a journalist with the *Sentinel*. With his coppery hair, Noah had defied the coloring shared by the other Whittakers, but he did share his brothers' height, easily topping six feet. Kayla was his perfect foil, a cute blonde with hair falling in a curtain past her shoulders.

Making up the end of the row were Matt's younger sister, Allison, whose cases as an Assistant District Attorney sometimes hit the papers, and her husband, Connor Rafferty, who owned his own security company.

Allison and Connor made an arresting couple, Lauren thought. Allison had the long dark hair, blue eyes and alabaster complexion of a china doll, and Connor had the sandy hair and manly good looks of an action hero.

Lauren hadn't expected to see the Whittakers here, and she definitely didn't expect them to descend on her once the show was over.

"Quent and I came as a show of support for Matt," Noah said with a grin as they all joined her at the end of the show.

"Romans come to watch a gladiator do battle is more like it," Allison countered.

Quentin smiled. "If your brothers aren't entitled to do some ribbing, who is?"

"Poor Matt," Kayla said.

Noah arched a brow. "Poor Matt, nothing. The guy has it coming to him."

"Yeah," Quentin put in, "I recall he was *really* sympathetic when Noah and I were having our own problems with women."

Elizabeth blinked. "You needed sympathy?"

Quent slung an arm around his wife's shoulders. "Er—only because I was in danger of losing the most wonderful woman in the world."

Allison threw her brother an arch look.

"So how is Matt doing?" Connor asked.

"He was wonderful, don't you think?" Lauren responded in what she hoped was an enthusiastic—but not *too* enthusiastic—voice. "I'm so glad he agreed to help us out today."

Quent and Noah exchanged amused looks.

"That's Matt," Quentin said. "The epitome of charitable largesse, especially when it comes to doing a favor for a, ah, friend."

"Yeah, our brother the male model," Noah added with a laugh. "Matt's hidden talents never fail to surprise."

Allison rolled her eyes. "Oh, cut it out, you two."

"Right, on to better stuff," Noah rejoined. "How's Matt doing on the dating circuit?"

"He's discussed it with you?" Lauren couldn't keep the note of surprise from her voice.

"Nothing is sacred between brothers," Noah said solemnly.

Catching the glint in Noah's eyes, she replied, "Maybe not, but some things are between me and my client, so *no comment.*"

The Whittaker women smiled, and Lauren could sense their approval for not bending to Noah's teasing.

"Now I know Matty Boy could have had a career as a male model," Noah continued unperturbed, "I think it'd have been easier if you'd just held a bachelor auction." A slow grin spread over his face. "You know, just let him go to the highest bidder."

She raised her eyebrows. "And I'm assuming you'd have wanted your take?"

"Sure, I'll claim my share of credit for making Matt what he is today," Noah deadpanned. "How do you think he got that scar on his jaw?"

"The same way you got the one at your hairline."

Lauren turned at the sound of Matt's voice.

He'd come up behind her, and she couldn't help her shiver of awareness.

She told herself again that her response was natural because he was big and male and any woman would feel petite and feminine in his presence. But the trouble with lying to herself was that there was no comfort in it.

Noah looked thoughtfully at his brother. "You know, if I could have predicted your future as a pretty boy, I'd have aimed to break your nose instead."

"I'd have liked to see you try," Matt replied dryly, before looking down at her. "Are they giving you a hard time?"

The question was stated casually, but there was an undertone of protective concern in his voice, as if he was worried his brother's teasing might be too much for her to handle.

The rational part of her wanted to tell him she was

more than capable of holding her own, but the feminine part of her went all soft and yielding.

"Yeah, we've been teasing her," Noah said.

"Then stop," Matt said curtly, his voice carrying a note of steel.

Lauren looked from one Whittaker brother to the other. Matt held his brother's gaze, his jaw set, while Noah met him head-on.

To her surprise, though, none of the other Whittakers looked bothered by the exchange.

Noah tilted his head, then said easily, "No problem." After a beat, he murmured, "If that's how the wind blows…"

Was Noah suggesting she and Matt were a couple? Until today, if anyone had asked, she would have said nothing could be further from the truth.

But after several hours of watching women gawk at Matt, her resistance to him had hit a new low.

And a voice whispered that the only reason Matt had participated today was for her. Why else brave his brothers' teasing and the relentless scrutiny of the press corps? Why else risk denting his image as a no-nonsense, steely corporate tycoon?

Sure, he was on the hunt for a wife, but he'd recently made it clear that he wanted *her*.

A guy who was willing to put himself and his reputation on the line that way for her was worth taking risks for, wasn't he?

She chewed her lip. She was about to make the best—or worst—decision of her life.

* * *

In the space of a day, Lauren reflected, she'd gone from an unattached woman, settled with a feline, to a woman looking for love in all the wrong places—in particular, in Matthew Whittaker's penthouse.

Matt had picked her up tonight after work and they'd driven to his apartment ostensibly to help him add some softening touches to his place. But she knew the truth. If ever there was a woman in danger of falling into the abyss, it was her.

She was a nervous wreck—so aware of him that his every movement practically made her jump. She had no experience making the first move, but acting normally while the air sizzled between them was next to impossible.

After ordering in and eating a quick dinner, they sat in Matt's living room, having unearthed his personal possessions from the boxes in his closets. Out came hockey trophies from high school and college, and out came mementos from his vacations in Australia and Myanmar. They also uncovered framed photos of family holidays.

Lauren studied one photo of Matt and the rest of the Whittakers standing in front of a Christmas tree. She recognized Matt's parents, Ava and James Whittaker, from passing acquaintance and photos in the newspapers. Ava, she knew, had gone back to school to get a law degree and was now a family court judge. James still sat as head of the board of directors of Whittaker Enterprises.

"That one was taken two years ago," Matt said.

She looked up. "It's a good shot."

She knew it had to be a recent photo. Quentin and Elizabeth's baby was in the picture. It was the sort of photo a woman hunting for a husband would like to see in a guy's apartment. The type of photo *she* liked to see.

It explained a lot about why Matt would be looking for a wife. The Whittakers made an attractive, happy family—the type of Norman Rockwell tableau anyone would be proud to display on their mantel. The sole person not paired up was Matt.

"It's from my pre-MEB days," Matt said.

In response to her questioning look, his lips quirked up, and he explained, "MEB—Most Eligible Bachelor days."

She felt his smile down to her toes, but she looked at the frame again and ran her fingers along the inlaid wood. "This frame is just right for the photo."

"That's my sister and sisters-in-law's doing. They know better than to give me anything that's not ready to set out."

"Lucky you."

She'd brought along a few photo frames of her own, just in case. After her first visit to his apartment, he'd okayed her purchase of some decorative items. Now she'd placed a photo frame here, a vase there, an interesting fluted bowl somewhere else.

It was the first time she'd gone shopping for a client.

"Go to Tiffany," he'd said, "and just bill it to my account."

She'd been thinking more along the lines of Bloomingdale's or Macy's, not quite so high-end but still elegant. In the end, though, she'd gone along with his suggestion. It was his money, after all, and she knew he had plenty of it.

The shopping trip had been reminiscent of her time spent putting together her bridal registry. Except then she'd been shopping for her future husband, and this time, well, it had been like feathering a love nest for her lover.

She'd come this evening dressed down—sort of— in jeans, practical heels and a clingy pink cashmere sweater. Work attire, or *seduce-me* wear, depending on how you looked at it. After all, she'd come to work, and, well—she hoped or feared—maybe something else.

He, not surprisingly, was dressed in Levi's. Stealing a surreptitious look at him, she noted he still managed to look commanding in an open-collar green shirt.

A tremor of sexual awareness went through her, then, restless, she got up to place the photo in her hand on a nearby side table.

Matt took the opportunity to sweep her an appreciative look.

She saw the look, and the photo frame slipped from her nerveless fingers. Matt caught it before it hit the floor.

In the same fluid motion, he stood up, his body brushing hers in the tight space between the couch and coffee table.

"Here—"

"No, I—"

They both stopped, the air between them pulsating with suppressed desires.

This was what she had come for.

She caught his raw male scent—soap and clean skin and just a whiff of shaving lotion—and the feminine core of her responded like a bee to nectar.

He lowered the photo frame, and her outstretched hand fell away from it at the same time.

"Where were you planning to put it?" he murmured, his eyes never leaving hers.

Her heart drummed in her ears.

"On the side table," she said, her voice breathy.

He nodded consideringly. "Good choice."

"You don't want the cluttered photo frame look. Just a touch is enough."

Her body cried out for him to touch her. *Now.*

"Uh-huh," he said, his voice thick.

She wet her lips, and like a laser, his eyes homed in on the movement.

"Does—does your offer still stand?"

He gave her a half-lidded look. "Depends on what offer we're talking about."

He was going to make her say it.

Her lips parted, but the words refused to come.

He slowly raised his free hand. With the backs of his fingers, he stroked down her cheek and the side of her neck.

She turned her face into the caress.

Not looking at him, she said in a low voice, "I'm talking about the offer to explore the attraction between us."

She was willing to take what came.

"I thought you'd never ask," he murmured.

He dropped the photo frame on the couch, and bent and kissed her.

The kiss was sure, thorough and consuming.

His hands cupped her shoulders and pulled her toward him, and for the first time she felt what it was like to be pressed against his long, hard masculine frame.

She wanted his encompassing heat as he deepened the kiss and it went on and on.

When he finally broke away, he bent and swept her up in his arms.

She was cradled high against his chest, her arm draped around his neck as his legs ate up the space between the living room and the back of the penthouse.

When they reached the master suite, he lowered her to the king-size bed, and its sumptuous bedding buoyed her—like an angel held aloft on a puffy cloud.

She had a passing impression of being surrounded by overpowering masculinity before he came down beside her.

He kissed her throat and caressed her thigh.

She looked up at the ceiling above her. A glimmer of doubt skittered along the edges of her mind.

She closed her eyes against it.

She could do this. She yearned for him.

It wouldn't be like the other times. She could will her body to take and give the pleasure he was showing her.

"Relax," he muttered against her throat. "Relax."

But his words had the opposite of their intended effect, and she stiffened further.

Her mind raced, trying to remember the thoughts that had brought her here—the edge of the cliff— where she usually balked.

Nothing was different. Not really.

How many times had Parker told her to *relax,* his voice holding a note of growing frustration?

Her thoughts picked up speed.

She'd been crazy to think she could tangle with a man like Matthew Whittaker. He was sophisticated, wealthy and experienced. Yes, he might appear wooden to the casual observer, but underneath lay a potent, sensual man.

And she was bound to disappoint, like an amateur cook at an *Iron Chef* competition.

"Stop."

The word tore from her.

To his credit, he drew back immediately and rolled to her side.

She bolted to a sitting position, and looked down at him.

His chest rose and fell, his breathing slowing.

He spoke first. "What's the matter?"

"I can't do this."

A puzzled frown marred his brow. "What do you mean?"

"I...I mean—" what *did* she mean? "—it's not what I want."

"You came to that conclusion only once we were horizontal and tangled on the bed together?"

He could also have added *painfully aroused,* she thought as her eyes slipped past the bulge in his pants, but she was glad he didn't.

"I'm sorry," she said lamely.

He frowned and sat up. "What is this? Some sort of game? One of your matchmaker tests to see if I can stop when the woman says no?"

When she made no response, his face changed, confusion hardening to anger and suspicion. "Or was this some little scheme of yours?"

"What do you mean?" she asked.

"I mean," he said coolly, "did you set it up so you could threaten to run to the newspapers with a story about my unwanted advances?"

"What? No! How could you even think such a thing?" She stood up, needing the space between, tugging at her twisted clothing.

"I'm a target," he went on ruthlessly. "A walking meal ticket in some women's eyes. Get something unsavory on me, and I can be hit up for hush money. I hired you to make sure those were the type of women I *didn't* meet."

He thought she was trying to blackmail him? His accusation left her breathless with outrage.

But then again, it was her own fault for getting involved with him.

Her experience with Parker should have taught her all about men like Matthew Whittaker.

"Running to the press would undermine everything you hired me to do," she said, her tone frosty. "I mean, it would hardly help you attract the perfect woman if you had the reputation of being a snake, now would it?"

He stood up, reversing the height difference between them, and making her conscious once again of just how big and male he was.

"You took me on as a client because of the money," he said, his eyes narrowing. "Maybe you realized there was an even easier way to earn some cash."

She didn't bother to deny the first half of his statement. She *had* taken him as a client because of the money—not to mention the publicity and recognition. She was just surprised he'd realized it, too, and had hired her anyway.

Still, the fact he'd gotten it halfway right did nothing to lessen her outrage. "If that's what you believe, then I'm more convinced than ever I don't belong here."

She tugged down her top, then looked around for her shoes. She spotted one peeking out from under the bed, and picked up the other from where it was lying on its side on the rug.

The act of dressing reminded her of what they'd been doing moments before, and brought a hot heat to her face.

"I'll drive you back," he said tersely.

"That's not necessary." She wouldn't look at him.

"You're not walking out of here alone at this hour." His voice was hard and commanding.

"I'll manage," she retorted.

She could ask the doorman to hail her a cab. "I wouldn't want you to risk a *compromising* situation by driving me back."

He ignored her. "I'll call you my car and driver."

At her raised eyebrows, he added, "I have one on call. All the top executives at Whittaker do. I use one to get to and from the airport when I fly for business."

Minutes later, when they got down to the lobby, the driver was waiting for her.

As the car pulled away from the curb, she glanced out the darkened passenger window to see Matt standing on the street, hands thrust into trouser pockets, a brooding expression on his face.

Only when the driver turned a corner, however, did she let the tears flow.

Seven

Matt leaned back in the leather armchair and gazed at the Boston skyline visible from his living room window. He swirled a snifter of brandy, downed a taste and set the glass down again on the armrest.

An hour or so ago, Lauren had run out of here as if the devil were nipping at her heels.

At the time, his adrenaline had been flowing. He'd been aroused, revved up and ready to go. Naturally when she'd said *stop,* his frustration had been at its peak.

Now, though, he could try to assess what had happened with a cooler head. Of course, he didn't believe she'd been trying to blackmail him. Those words had come flying out of him because he'd been confronted by a situation that didn't make sense and had been suffering from a sizable amount of frustrated desire.

One minute she'd been soft and pliant in his arms, the next she'd gone rigid and withdrawn.

Something had gotten to Lauren, and the change had been so abrupt; so thorough—like a flip of the switch—that he was willing to bet money now that whatever it was, it predated his arrival on the scene, or at least, his arrival this second time around.

He wondered whether Parker's jilting had done this to her—this lack of confidence—and his gut tightened at the thought.

Not that he had any experience with this sort of thing, but he figured something like getting stood up at the altar could have undermined Lauren's confidence as a woman—no matter how desirable and attractive she was.

And she was lovely. She made him ache just looking at her. He had trouble being in the same room with her without his sex drive roaring up to speed like a race car. He wanted to topple onto the couch with her—no, scratch that, they'd never even make it there, it would have to be the floor instead—and make passionate love.

The fact he'd had the fortitude to carry her to his bed earlier in the evening was a miracle. He'd gone from zero to sixty in under a minute, so turned-on had he been by her. That hadn't happened to him with any other woman.

He tilted his head and stared at the twinkling lights of Boston. On second thought, maybe *that* had been the problem. Maybe she'd sensed his barely leashed desire, and it had brought her insecurities to the surface, scaring her off.

He raised his glass and took another gratifying swill. There was always the possibility, of course, that her reaction in the bedroom had been happening even *before* her almost wedding to Parker.

Now that was an interesting thought. Good ol' Parker as less than a satisfactory lover, but too much of a gentleman to admit to it.

Sure, it took two to tango, but in Matt's experience with women, he'd learned there were plenty of men who didn't know or didn't care about their partner's pleasure.

Of course, he thought ruefully, he was one to talk. His performance earlier this evening hadn't been too far from setting its own speed record because he'd been so hot to have Lauren.

He had to set things straight between them. She didn't deserve the words he'd given her. And he needed to understand what had happened tonight as much as she did. He wanted her too much to do anything else.

"I don't want to talk about it." *Him.* I mean, *him,* Lauren corrected in her mind.

It had become her mantra. Unfortunately, Candace hadn't heard it enough. How else to explain why her receptionist continued to bring up Matt?

She and Candace were having lunch in Ideal Match's reception area, having picked up soups and salads from a nearby deli, and already Candace had mentioned Matt three times.

Ever since Candace had walked in on her and Matt on that rainy day almost two weeks ago, she'd persisted in bringing him up, evidently in some deluded quest to make her Boston's Most Envied Bride, as if Matt were some trophy and she were a lead contender in the prize tournament.

Actually, Matt *was* a trophy, but the only thing she wanted was his framed shot on her wall, above a caption alluding to Ideal Match's biggest success story to date.

Of course, she hadn't heard from Matt since Sunday, when she'd dashed out of his apartment. For all she knew, he no longer considered himself her client.

Given what a flaming disaster her attempt at playing the seductress had been, she now couldn't consider him as anything more.

But then again, she was crazy to consider him as anything *at all*. He'd made some unforgivable comments.

She stabbed her fork into her salad with more force than necessary, then hoped Candace hadn't noticed.

She hadn't told Candace anything about Sunday night and her angry exchange with Boston's leading single. She didn't want her receptionist making some snide comment when Matt called—*if* he called.

At least, she liked to think that was the reason she was keeping information from Candace, and not that she was desperate to see Matt again despite everything.

As far as her receptionist was concerned, she and Matt were still at the point where they had crossed the threshold of civilized behavior when they'd been tangled together on the reception desk.

She grew hot now recalling their passionate encounter then. She hadn't felt panicked, probably because Candace's unexpected return had prevented her from getting to that inevitable moment.

"You're crazy," Candace said, recalling her to the present.

As if she needed confirmation, Lauren thought gloomily.

Candace chewed and waved her fork. "I mean, Matt is gorgeous, wealthy and obviously a tiger in bed." She made a growling sound. "Yours to tame, sweetie."

Lauren rolled her eyes. "What is this? A discussion of my personal life or a commercial for the circus?"

"Stay on topic."

"I don't want to tame anything." *Him.* Especially, *him.* She wouldn't even know how. But she'd never gone there with Candace, and she wouldn't start now.

Candace shook her head. "And what do you do instead? You keep trying to hook the poor guy up with other women."

"It's what pays the rent."

"Hon, you've been doing this matchmaking gig too long," Candace said. "Love is an event of first come, first serve, and I'm here to tell you, serve yourself first, sweetie. Particularly when the guy's a yummy dish like Matt Whittaker."

"Too spicy for my taste."

Candace, in the process of lifting the fork to her mouth, stopped in midmotion, the look of surprise on her face quickly replaced by one that was wicked. "*Well.*"

Lauren knew she'd skirted the line of revealing too much, but *not* in the way Candace plainly thought.

"I thought the problem was he was too bland," Candace said.

"I think what I said was, too starchy in the collar."

Candace grinned. "It's always the buttoned-down silent types…"

She wondered what Candace would say if she shared details of Sunday night—Matt's accusations, the upsetting things he'd said, and yet the brooding look on his face when her car had pulled away.

She hadn't been able to put the last out of her mind.

She now had a failed seduction as well as a failed wedding under her belt. Terrible for anyone, but more than depressing for a professional matchmaker.

She ought to stamp her letterhead with the word *phony* and be done with it, she thought gloomily.

* * *

She ordinarily didn't meet clients at her apartment. She liked to keep her work separate from her personal space, as much as possible, but it wasn't as if Matt was just a client.

She'd never almost had sex with a client before, Lauren thought. She'd never even come close because she'd never had a romantic relationship with one. She'd never had more than dinner to hone a client's social skills.

But Matt had insisted he needed to talk to her, and she hadn't felt like waiting around her office until eight, or whenever his business dinner ended.

He'd suggested his schedule was otherwise full this week, and anyway, she figured she should just get this meeting over with.

She expected he was coming to tell her his days as a client of Ideal Match were over. This was the last time she'd have to fit in an appointment to meet him.

She was dressed in jeans and a beige microchenille cardigan paired with stack-heeled mules. Her hair was pulled back in a ponytail, and she'd removed her makeup when she'd gotten home from work and eaten dinner. She refused to let herself primp for Matt's arrival.

In the days since she and Matt had almost made love at his apartment, her anger had ebbed, replaced by resignation and defeat. But it was hard to characterize the other emotions churning within her.

And then he was there, ringing her buzzer—no fancy doorman for her—and she was opening her door to a Matt who still had snowflakes clinging to the shoulders of his overcoat and who looked steely yet gorgeous.

"Thanks for meeting me on such short notice—"

"Let me take your coat," she said on the tail end of his words.

She wouldn't let him slip under her armor again. She wouldn't let him suspect how the tears had seeped from under her eyelids as she lay in bed at night.

After he'd discarded his coat and she'd hung it up in the hall closet, he held out a brown paper bag.

"This is for you," he said. "A peace offering."

"Thank you."

She was stumped as to what he could have brought, but she took the bag from him anyway and peeked inside.

"Healthy gourmet cat food," he said. "Candace mentioned at one point that you have a cat."

Lauren wondered what else Candace had been telling Matt. "Thank you. Felix will be appreciative."

As a goodwill gesture, it wasn't bad. Perhaps he *had* learned something from her coaching.

Aloud, she said approvingly, "Cat food is an imaginative gift to give a woman."

Then belatedly realizing the multiple ways he could interpret her comment, she could have bitten off her tongue.

But he appeared not to notice.

"I've learned a number of things," he said.

She went motionless, and he stood there, handsome in a charcoal suit, his expression heavy.

"I said some things to you I didn't mean," he said flatly.

She fought an involuntary smile. In typical guy fashion, he was coming as close as possible to an apology without actually saying the word *sorry*. Maybe he hadn't changed so much after all.

He looked around. "Where's Felix? It occurred to me on the way over that this is the first time I've been here. You came down to the car when I picked you up for Veronica and Albert's wedding."

"That's right." She looked around. "Felix often hides out in my bedroom."

"Lucky cat."

She got goose bumps. She couldn't help herself. He said it so matter-of-factly but with such certainty.

"I'm taking heart in the fact there's still one male you like," he joked.

"Felix has been neutered," she said in a deadpan voice.

His lips twitched. "Ouch."

She turned toward her bedroom. "You might as well get the grand tour, though there's not much to see. It's a typical one-bedroom apartment."

He nodded, looking around. "But sentimentally decorated."

She cast him a look from the corner of her eyes. "You mean, unlike your palatial spread?"

He smiled at her gibe. "Hardly a palace, but yeah, in contrast to my place. Though thanks to you, these days my condo is looking a lot better."

"The kitchen is off the foyer, where you entered." She waved to her right. "And off this short hallway is the bathroom and bedroom."

She tried to see the apartment through his eyes. The furnishings were simple but elegant and feminine. She'd hunted long and hard for furniture that was compact, not wanting to overwhelm her small place.

The main room was a combination living room and dining room, with a small blond dinette table near the foyer and a comfortable deep-cushioned sofa and leather armchair near the windows at the opposite end. Carved fretwork lined the edges of the coffee table she'd bought at a flea market. Framed photos occupied a couple of side tables, and a bookcase stood against the far wall.

After a moment, she headed into the bedroom, and Matt followed. She could almost feel the heat he radiated as if the sun were on her back.

She spotted Felix napping in the middle of her red-and-white toile bedcover.

"So this is the famous Felix," Matt said from behind her.

Felix opened his eyes, then stretched.

"I picked him up at a shelter after…"

She'd almost said, after she got back from her honeymoon trip with her sister, but she'd stopped herself.

"Yes, Candace told me."

She watched as Matt bent to pet her orange tabby, but Felix jumped down and rubbed himself against Matt's trouser legs.

"He's a tiger," she said wryly.

Matt chuckled. "Yeah, I can see that."

After a moment, Felix ambled out of the room, and she said, "He must have sensed the treat you brought him."

She glanced around her room and wondered again at the impression her apartment made on Matt. Her bedroom furniture was cherrywood with rattan cane accents, neither frilly nor spare. She'd treated herself to it as a reward for making Ideal Match a small success.

Matt watched Felix depart, then his eyes came back to hers.

Silence reigned. Palpable, hot and sexually charged.

They'd danced around the issues long enough, and they both knew it.

"Why—"

"Let's—"

They both started speaking at once, then stopped.

He nodded for her to go ahead.

She rubbed damp palms against her jeans and suppressed a nervous laugh.

Matt Whittaker in her bedroom. Life rarely got more surprising.

She wet her lips and took a deep breath. "Why are you here?"

A nerve jumped in his jaw. "To tell you I'd take back what I said if I could. I know you aren't looking for a quick payoff."

"But you want to be let out of your deal with Ideal Match," she jumped in.

"Yes—"

Her stomach plummeted.

"I mean, no." He raked his fingers through his hair in frustration.

Her stomach plunged further. It was crazy. She still both did and didn't want him as a client. She was both angry at him and yet yearning for him.

At the same time, in the back of her mind, she noted she'd never seen Matt Whittaker so frustrated.

Then she thought back to their last encounter and corrected herself. Well, *maybe* on one other occasion.

"I don't want to date Bethany or Melanie or Valerie," he said flatly.

"We've already established that."

"I don't want to date women you think Parker would have liked to marry."

She opened her mouth, then clamped it shut. The words were harsh, brutal…and true.

"I want you."

Her heart leaped. "I'm not available."

He looked around. "Why? Felix is the jealous type?"

"Felix is a cat. He leads a solitary existence."

"Then what's the problem?"

She didn't want to say. It was intimate stuff, and she'd be exposed as a fraud.

He walked toward her. "Once burned, twice shy?"

"You could say so."

He set his hands at her waist.

"Then let's take it from the top," he said gently.

She must have looked worried, because he added, "It's been a while for you?"

"Since the wedding." The admission slipped out.

He registered no surprise. "We'll take it slow."

He bent his head, and she knew he was going to kiss her. He stopped, however, and searched her face for a moment.

When his mouth did meet hers, it was just a feathery brush of the lips, but enough to make her shiver.

It was the first dash of color on a blank canvas, where he was the artist and she was his creation.

He moved his lips softly and gently, nibbling away at her tension, his hands stroking up and down her arms.

She sighed as some of her anxiety left her. Parker had never had the patience to go slow.

They stood there like that for the longest time.

Lifting his head finally, he murmured, "I read somewhere that sex for women is in the brain."

"Mmm."

There was a slight swaying, lulling motion to their embrace.

He rained little kisses over her face as his hands

went to the pearlized snaps of her cardigan, gently pulling them apart.

Sensing her slight stiffening, he murmured against her temple, "Shh. Trust me."

He undressed her leisurely, telling her how beautiful she was and how desirable he found her.

Along the way, she pushed his suit jacket off his shoulders and let it slip to the floor.

"That's right," he encouraged in a low voice. "Show me what you want."

He loosened his tie and tossed it aside, then set to work on his cuff links and the buttons of his shirt.

When he pulled off the shirt, he revealed the hard, lean, sun-kissed expanse of his chest.

"Touch me," he urged.

And she did, admiring the way the light and shadows cast by the bedside lamp highlighted the smooth muscles of his arms and chest.

The hard bulge beneath his belt gave her pause, but when her eyes traveled back up to his, he said quietly, "I want you."

She thought about being possessed by him and shivered with awareness. Five years ago, he'd been a remote stranger at the periphery of her life, but had still, even then, managed to evoke a deep, primal response from her—one she'd been reluctant to acknowledge at the time.

Now was a different matter, though, and she couldn't hide the signs of how he affected her. She felt small and delicate next to him, but rather than being daunted by the difference in their size, she was turned on by it.

He picked her up and laid her on the bed. Then he retrieved a tube from the pocket of his suit jacket, as well as a familiar-looking foil packet.

At her questioning look, he said, "Massage."

She'd never had a massage before. Just the thought of his hands kneading her all over sent her senses into overload.

She watched as he squeezed some sweet-smelling lotion from the tube and rubbed it between his hands.

"Apparently," he said conversationally, as if he wasn't about to get to know her inch by inch, "the use of massage oils contributes to the calming and soothing benefits of the massage."

"Really?" she croaked as he kneeled beside her on the bed.

He arched a brow. "Are you going to turn over?"

She hesitated.

"I dare you." Then he nodded at her underwear. "Bra and panties optional."

She was scared of disappointing, but also so turned-on her fingers were shaking.

In the end, rampant need won out, and she fumbled with the clasp of her bra.

When the bra fell away from her—the rustle loud in the silence—he sucked in a breath, his pupils large, his eyes dark.

"Lovely," he murmured.

She slipped off her underwear and flipped over before she lost her courage.

He straddled her and placed his hands on her back.

A ripple of sensation went through her.

"I've been told," he said, his voice low, "the secret to a great massage is confident hands."

His hands stroked down her spine toward the middle of her back, then swiveled outward toward the sides of her rib cage, before coming back up again.

"This is called an effleurage stroke," he said as he repeated the motion. "It's to loosen up and soothe."

He went through the motion again and again, his rhythm hypnotic.

She sighed. She didn't care what they called it. It was heavenly.

His hands shifted direction, massaging in a spiraling circle, first on one side of her body, then on the other.

She felt herself unwind. The massage felt *wonderful.*

"When did you learn to do this?" she said, her voice muffled as she rested her head on her crossed arms.

He gave a quiet laugh. "Yesterday. I'm trying out my technique for the first time."

She lifted her head and glanced over her shoulder at him. "Yesterday?"

"I bought a book on massage therapy and flipped through it last night."

She turned back around and laid her face sideways on her hands. "You were planning this?"

"Let's just say I was hopeful." He added, "If you'd been around when I was reading, I never would have gotten to the end. The urge to test out the instructions would have been irresistible."

She wondered how she should feel about his planning this, then decided she was feeling too good to bother continuing to analyze it.

She felt loose. His magical hands lulled her into a state in which she was both acutely aware and yet entranced by what he was doing.

His thumbs pressed along her spine, working their way down in small circular motions.

"This," he said, "is a petrissage stroke. It releases tension."

Umm was all she could think.

He used similar moves on one leg, then on the other. "They're techniques of Swedish massage."

"Umm." She took a deep breath. "I have Swedish ancestry."

"A petite brunette like you?"

She heard the smile in his voice.

"I know it's hard to believe," she responded. "The rest is a mix of Welsh and French. What about you?"

"Pure Boston blue blood," he admitted, his tone regretful. "One predecessor came over on the *Mayflower.*"

"Just one?"

"Well, that's if you don't count the rumored infidelities."

She smiled.

"So, I'm curious," he said. "What have you learned from these years of being a matchmaker?"

"About?" She nearly moaned as his fingers worked at a knot near her shoulder blades.

"About the difference between men and women."

She could feel his arousal and thought fleetingly about giving him the obvious answer. "You really want to know?"

"I really want to," he said in confirmation.

"Well…after an argument, women are too upset to have sex, while men *only* want to have sex."

She heard him laugh low in his throat.

She sighed. "This is wonderful."

"I could've used massage toys, but I prefer to use my hands."

She had no complaints about his hands.

He leaned in and asked, "What was that?"

Realizing she must have spoken out loud, she mumbled, "No complaints."

His hands were square and firm. Perfect.

After what seemed like hours, he turned her over and massaged her from the front, starting with her feet and working his way up, using his lips as well as his hands.

An eon passed, and she drifted in and out of sensible thought, moaning as he did incredible things to her.

Each time she thought he would take her,

however, he found another part of her to fascinate him.

"Feel good?" he said thickly, once or twice.

"Yes," she responded, her voice breathy and shallow.

"Remember, learn to ask for what you want."

And she did, slowly, hesitantly, but gradually with more confidence. At one point, he used some lubrication, and if possible, she relaxed even more.

Eventually, he rolled to his side, and she heard the rustle of foil being ripped.

She felt like wax melting around a candle, and he braced himself on his arms above her.

"Okay?" he said hoarsely.

She was too boneless to make a coherent reply, causing him to chuckle.

He positioned himself and entered her slowly, giving her time and letting them savor the moment.

It was lovely, she thought hazily. Rather than a tumultuous storm tossing waves onto bleak cliffs, this was a joyous roller-coaster ride under sun showers.

He kissed her long and deep. His hands were everywhere, touching, soothing and sampling the texture of her skin and bringing her to life in her most secret places until, suddenly and unexpectedly, her senses rioted and she blossomed like a flower under the sun.

Eight

Matt gritted his teeth and hung on to his control.

As soon as he felt Lauren's release, however, his mind shut down and primal instinct took over.

His release came hard and fast. Dimly, he was aware of Lauren's moans mingling with his own sounds of pleasure.

Afterward, they lay spent, side by side.

He looked over at her, sweat still slicking his skin.

Her eyes were closed, her lips still puffy.

"So," he said, after his heart had resumed its normal rhythm, "any areas I need to improve?"

Her eyes fluttered open, and she fixed him with those incredible sea-green eyes of hers.

"None I can think of," she said, her voice husky.

"How were the kisses?" he asked.

She cleared her throat. "Er—excellent."

He rolled onto his side to face her, and she turned to face him.

He let the back of one hand caress her leisurely but kept pushing. "Massage?"

"Expert."

"Caresses?" he probed.

"Wonderful."

"Pacing?"

She searched his face. "Experienced."

"Orgasm?"

She wet her lips. "Registered high on the Richter scale."

"Good." A powerful shot of possessiveness went through him.

"It's never…registered before," she said. "With, umm, Parker."

She cleared her throat. "There was no one else."

"Ah." Understanding dawned, and with it, a primal possessiveness.

So, he'd guessed right. Not only had Lauren been celibate for a long time, but things with Parker had been nothing to brag about.

Yet, she was the one with the angst, while Parker—wherever he was—was probably walking around with his usual bravado.

He leashed his anger and gathered Lauren close.

"Well, for the record, the sex tonight was mind-blowing."

Her eyes widened. "Really?"

The earnest expression on her face almost killed him. "Yes, *really.*"

"I didn't know it could be so good." She stopped and bit her lip in an endearing way. "I mean I knew it could be that good. I've read about it. I just didn't know it could be so good *for me.*"

"Sometimes unbridled passion overcomes our inhibitions."

"I doubt I have any inhibitions left."

He grinned. "Who knows how these things work? Maybe sex with Parker would have been better if you'd felt more comfortable."

She sighed. "Yes."

"I'm glad the massage worked."

She raised her head to look at him. "I can't believe you skimmed a massage book!"

He grinned again. "Are you kidding? A visit to the sex toys shop was going to be the next step."

She laughed.

He pretended to be offended. "What's so funny?"

"You, staid and intimidating Matthew Whittaker, in a sex toys shop."

He nodded. "The Pink Kitten. A man's gotta do what a man's gotta do." Then he frowned. "And what do you mean *staid?*"

For effect, he let his hand trail over her breast and down to the sensitive hollow of her hip.

She flushed. "Well…except now I know you're not at all staid—"

He moved quickly, not giving her time to react, and flipped her over him.

She gasped. "What are you doing?"

He gave her a wicked look. "Well, we haven't scored *stamina* yet."

She glanced over at the bedside clock. "You need to go to work in the morning."

"I have a shower at my office, and I always keep an extra suit lying around."

At her raised eyebrows, he added, "Not to worry, sweetheart. It's not because I'm such a Casanova, but for those days when I go straight to the office off the red-eye from Silicon Valley."

Then he made sure neither of them were talking for a very long time.

Lauren hummed.

"Someone's in a good mood," Candace said, entering her office with a package.

Lauren smiled. "It's a beautiful day."

It had been two weeks since Matt's visit to her apartment, and things had only gotten better between them. Both in bed and out. They could barely be in the same room together without fogging up windows.

She grew hot just thinking about all the times and all the places they'd been intimate.

In a desperate effort to get to work on time, they'd showered together, but even then things had often taken an unexpected turn.

No doubt about it. She was a new Lauren
Fletcher—more sure of herself sexually with every
passing day. And she had Matt Whittaker to thank for
it. He'd broken down her barriers. Just a couple of
months ago, she'd never have guessed her new path.

Since Parker had been her first lover, she hadn't
known how much more to expect because she hadn't
known how much she'd been missing.

Candace eyed her. "Mmm-hmm. Well, just for the
record, remember I argued you should have given in
to that man a long time ago."

"Remind me to get you a gift."

She'd spilled the beans to Candace that she and
Matt were really a couple. Her receptionist would
have figured it out for herself soon enough anyway,
because Ideal Match was no longer making finding
dates for Matt a priority.

Yes, she'd given up Ideal Match's prime candidate, but she'd gain so much more besides. She was
willing to jump in with both feet and see where
things between her and Matt led, because she was no
longer afraid.

"Here." Candace handed her the box she was
holding and pretended to look perplexed. "It just
arrived by messenger. I wonder who it's from."

She felt giddy. "Let's see."

She opened the box and pushed aside the tissue
paper inside. Her heart skipped a beat as she pulled
out a beautiful gown of green satin.

Holding it up, she noticed it had rhinestone straps

and starburst pleats that fanned out from the bust, where a rhinestone clasp nestled.

"He's getting good, really good," Candace said.

Lauren picked up and scanned the accompanying note. *Wear this for me.* Matt had signed his name and written a day and time. It was the night of the Grosvenor Gala Dinner in support of Boston's art museums that they had talked about.

Candace handed her a jewelry box. "Here, you missed this."

She opened it gingerly, and gasped. A simple diamond necklace, along with diamond stud earrings, nestled inside the box.

Candace bent forward for a peek, then gasped, as well.

"You are now officially a kept woman," her receptionist joked.

Lauren felt the tears escape. She'd wear everything—as well as her heart on her sleeve.

Because she loved him.

Candace patted her arm. "Hey, hey. It's time to crack open the bubbly, not the waterworks."

"Don't pay attention to me," she warbled.

"You know, if this one bails on you," Candace teased, "I'm guessing you'll get an even better deal from the pawnshop than you did for the engagement ring."

The Imperial Ballroom in the Boston Park Plaza Hotel glittered under the light reflected from several large crystal chandeliers.

The room, filled almost to capacity tonight with more than five hundred dinner guests, had an old-world elegance thanks to its vaulted ceiling, gilded balconies and ornate archways.

Lauren felt transported to a different time and place, captivated by the charm of her surroundings and even more so, by the man at her side.

She was wearing the dress Matt had sent her, having paired it with silver pumps and a silver clutch from her closet. Her hair was swept up, and she'd used a black cape to protect herself on the way over against the cold weather outside.

The ensemble boosted her confidence as they stood speaking with the other Whittakers.

She felt she could use all the confidence she could get. When she'd questioned Matt on the drive over, he'd responded that he hadn't outright told his family about their budding relationship.

He hadn't totally understood her distressed reaction, either.

"It's nerve-wracking enough that we'll be scrutinized by everybody else," she said, not even wanting to think about the reporters who would likely be at the Gala, "but couldn't you at least have warned your family in advance?"

"Everything will be fine," he responded, reaching out to give her hand a squeeze.

But she'd refused to be completely comforted.

She knew the Whittakers would have questions— at least voiced in their eyes, if not spoken. After all,

Matt's siblings knew she'd been his matchmaker, and before that, he'd been a groomsman at her almost wedding. Her history with Matt couldn't get more complicated.

And whereas before, they may have merely suspected something more than a platonic relationship existed between her and their brother, tonight she and Matt might as well have taken out on ad in the newspapers.

Still, she knew she loved Matt, and she couldn't hide her feelings and still be true to herself.

Matt's warm hand at the small of her back was reassuring as she faced his family, including his parents.

They were all standing next to the table where they would be seated for dinner in a short while.

Matt's mother, Ava, was graceful and gracious, her coiffed hair as dark as Matt's but tinged with gray. The resemblance to her daughter, Allison, was striking.

Matt's father, James, dressed in a tux like the other men, was tall and distinguished looking and possessed an easy charm.

"Matt mentioned you're a professional matchmaker, Lauren," Ava said.

"Er—yes." *His* matchmaker until recently, she wanted to point out.

"It must have been challenging to start your own business," James said.

"Yes, but rewarding, too," she responded. "I've been active in associations of women small business owners here in Boston."

She was relieved Matt's parents, at least, seemed too polite to bring up the subject of how precisely she'd transitioned from being their son's matchmaker to, from all appearances, being his lover.

His brothers were another story.

"So, Matt, how's the matchmaking thing going?" Noah asked later, when they had sat down to dinner.

Matt took his time responding. "I'm no longer in the market."

Noah cupped his hand to his ear. "What was that? I couldn't hear you."

"*I said* I'm no longer in the market."

Noah opened his eyes wide. "Not even Lauren could find someone to date you, huh?"

Quent stifled a chuckle.

"*Noah*," Ava warned, but the look Noah gave his mother was all innocence.

Lauren watched Matt lean back and drape an arm over the back of her chair. "Lauren *is* my date for tonight, in case it's escaped your notice."

Lauren caught the look of delighted approval Allison exchanged with Elizabeth and Kayla as their apparent suspicions were confirmed.

Noah feigned surprise. "You mean she isn't here just to make sure you're schooled in the social graces?"

"*No*."

It wasn't so much that Matt's brothers wanted to tease her, Lauren realized, as that they were intent on ribbing Matt in some time-honored family ritual.

"You mean she's here with you as a *real* date?" Noah persisted.

"As real as it gets," Matt drawled.

Lauren felt herself heat. Matt might as well have come out and announced that they'd been having spectacular sex together night after night.

She waited to be swallowed up by a large hole.

"You're both embarrassing Lauren," Allison said, "so stop."

Lauren threw her a grateful look.

It was then she noticed the other Whittakers were looking at her—not with suspicion, but with sympathy and, yes, kindness.

Her heart squeezed, and she blinked hard. She knew she'd just stepped over a significant threshold.

It was only later on the dance floor that she could express herself, however.

"I like your family," she said.

Matt looked down at her drolly. "It's nice of you to say so, but they can be a pain in the butt."

"Refreshing."

"Now there's a euphemism if ever I heard one."

She smiled. "No, they were welcoming."

He tilted his head as they made their way past another couple on the crowded dance floor. A twenty-piece orchestra played above them on the stage. "You say that as if you're surprised."

"Parker's family wasn't the same way," she said.

"Is that your way of saying they were wealthy and

snobby?" he asked, his voice laced with amusement but carrying a note of seriousness, as well.

"Distant and formal," she countered, struggling for words to explain. "Dinner at their house always ended with coffee and dessert. A plate with exactly one cookie for each person at the table."

He grinned. "They must have been some pricey cookies."

"I know it sounds ridiculous."

He shook his head, sobering. "No, Parker's family always struck me as rather arrogant."

"Well, let's just say they would have claimed ancestors on the *Mayflower* whether they were legitimate or not."

His eyes crinkled. "That's right, hit me where it hurts."

His face changed then, acquiring a quiet intensity. "I'm glad you wore the dress. You look fantastic."

Lauren raised a hand self-consciously to her throat. The diamond necklace felt cool against her skin. She was lucky the Whittakers didn't know who'd given it to her. As it was, they'd been more than a little curious—and amused—by her apparent love affair with the last single Whittaker.

"The gown is beautiful," she said. "So are the necklace and earrings, but they're too expensive for me to keep—"

He silenced her with a light kiss. "Let me convince you to keep them."

His voice was full of smoky promise, and Lauren shivered in response.

It was, she thought, a magical night. She felt swept away on a wave of frothy happiness.

Rather than looking forward to the evening's end, as she'd done in the car, it came all too soon for her.

In the lobby, they waited for Matt's car to be brought around. Other guests were departing from the Imperial Ballroom, and hotel guests went in and out.

Matt leaned close. "I can't wait to help you out of that dress."

A smile rose to her lips, and in the next second froze there.

Parker.

It took a moment for her mind to catch up with her senses.

She hadn't seen him in five years, but now he'd come out of the revolving doors and was striding through the lobby toward them, as casual as can be.

Following the direction of her gaze, Matt stiffened beside her.

In the next instant, Parker spotted them and his expression darkened. There was just a momentary break in his step, though, as he continued to move forward. He stopped only when he was face to face with them. "Well, this is a surprise," he drawled.

"Parker," Matt acknowledged, while Lauren remained frozen in place.

Parker's mouth curved into an unpleasant smile.

"I'd heard from some departing guests that you two were at the Gala together tonight, but there's nothing like seeing it for myself."

Lauren realized Parker was buzzed from a night on the town. His eyes were too bright, and the hollows under them shadowed.

Still, even taking into account his temporary worn state, it was clear the intervening years had not been good to Parker. He looked wasted in a way that went deeper than one night of carousing.

She wondered whether those signs had been there five years ago, or whether they were more recent symptoms of a life that had disappointed.

There was a weakness around his mouth, a sullen expression in his eyes and a spoiled look about his face.

"I guess it's a happy coincidence we ran into you then," Matt said dryly. "It's fascinating how far rumors can travel."

Parker's jaw worked. "I've been staying at the Park Plaza since getting back to Boston two days ago. At the time, I didn't realize I'd find my almost wife had fallen into the arms of one of my grooms-men."

"Hardly," Matt countered. "It's been five years. Five years in which you were incommunicado."

Lauren could feel the tension vibrating between the two men. The three of them were starting to attract curious stares from people around them.

Parker's lip curled. "Now I know why you talked

me into calling off the wedding. You wanted her for yourself, you bastard."

She stared at Parker uncomprehendingly.

Then she realized it wasn't that she *hadn't* comprehended what Parker was saying, it was that she *didn't* want to.

Matt instigating Parker to jilt her at the altar? *It couldn't be true.*

"If you have regrets, you've got only yourself to blame," Matt said, his tone cold. "We both know the real reason you called it off was that you weren't man enough to stand up to your family, and certainly not man enough to deserve Lauren."

Those were fighting words, and Lauren knew it.

Parker sprinted forward, but it was Matt who landed the first punch, and it was chaos after that.

They slammed into each other.

Around them, people gasped and moved themselves out of the way.

Lauren couldn't believe it. She couldn't believe the unflappable Matthew Whittaker was involved in a brawl…she couldn't believe he and Parker were landing blows…and she particularly couldn't believe they were fighting over *her.*

"Stop it!" she said, her voice sounding ineffectual to her own ears.

She looked frantically around her for help, but none of the other Whittakers were in sight and the middle-aged crowd appeared to be an unlikely source of assistance.

Her eyes darted back to the two combatants in time to see Matt deliver a blow that knocked Parker off his feet.

She winced, then saw her chance and dashed forward.

"That's enough!" She sounded shrill, bordering on hysterical.

A tremor ran through her as she grabbed Matt's arm and pulled him back from where he was standing over Parker. She managed to pull him only a half step, even after putting all her weight into it.

Staggering on the floor before them, Parker nursed a bloody lip, his clothing torn. He sported a couple of bruises on his face that promised to turn black-and-blue.

Glancing up at Matt, Lauren noticed he looked little better. Disheveled, his chest rising and falling with every breath, he had an angry bruise near his jaw. He was a far cry from the polished man she'd laughed and danced with earlier in the evening.

Parker's accusation flashed through her mind again.

Matt hadn't categorically denied it.

She again tried to digest the fact that Matt—her seducer, now her lover—might have been responsible for the worst humiliation of her life.

Just in time, though, hotel security arrived, making their way through the throng around them.

People whispered, and Lauren thought with mortification about how long it would take her to live this down. It had taken her five years to move on after the jilting.

As a security guard hoisted him up by one arm, Parker wiped his lip with the back of his hand. "I'll sue, you bastard. I'll make you sorry we ever crossed paths."

Another guard put a restraining arm in front of Matt's chest.

"You came after me," Matt responded in a clipped voice. "A lawsuit's not going to get you anywhere— even if you stay in town long enough to bring one."

Lauren looked at Matt. "Is it true? Is what Parker said true?"

He glanced down at her and said nothing, but she could read the answer in his eyes.

"We'll talk later," he said curtly.

She took a step back. He'd transformed once again into a stranger with hard blue eyes, a corporate tycoon with a will of steel.

Within moments, his siblings and their spouses arrived, peppering them with questions and exclamations of surprise.

She slipped away in the ensuing confusion. *She had to get away.*

"Lauren, wait!"

Matt's voice sounded behind her, but she just kept going. She knew he couldn't leave without explaining things to hotel security, though she was also sure Matt's wealth and social prominence would mean he was treated with deference and respect.

She, on the other hand, would be paying the price for tonight for a long time to come.

Outside the hotel, the March night greeted her with a cold blast, and she welcomed it. She needed to clear her head.

She asked a liveried bellhop to summon a cab, and luckily, one was on the scene in a couple of minutes. She avoided looking at anyone else, but she could feel the stares of those who'd obviously witnessed the debacle inside.

She got into the back of the cab, and as it took her home through Boston's darkened streets, a knot of dread lodged itself in her throat.

She leaned back and rested her head against the back of her seat. So much for her plan to cultivate Matt's image as a rich, refined bachelor that any woman would be happy to take home to her mother. Of course, *that* plan had recently been replaced by the one where *she* would be happy to take him home to *her* mother.

Still, if she hadn't scarred his reputation as an eligible bachelor by showing up on his arm tonight, then the run-in with Parker certainly had.

She was such a fool. She couldn't believe she even thought she might be falling in love.

Obviously, she hadn't learned anything in the past five years because she was repeating her mistakes.

She'd been wrong *again* to think she'd made an ideal match—*her* ideal match. Instead, she was once more Ms. First Runner-up.

She should have trusted her initial instincts instead of persuading herself to dismiss the superficial similarities between Matt and Parker.

Of course, *that* was before she knew of Matt's past betrayal and present deceitfulness. Now she knew the similarities between the two men ran to even more than the superficial. They were both untrustworthy snakes.

By tomorrow, gossip would be circulating, and the newspapers would be flashing headlines about the fight at the Boston Park Plaza—apparently over her.

Things were such a mess. She felt like weeping.

She paid the driver when he pulled to a stop in front of her apartment building, then got out, digging into her purse for her keys.

"Lauren."

She turned at the sound of Matt's voice, and her heart tripped over itself.

"How did you get here?" she blurted.

She watched him walk over to her from his car.

He was the last person she wanted to see right now. She was an emotional wreck. She might as well hang a sign on her heart that read Condemned.

Even disheveled and bruised, however, he was the most magnetic man she knew.

"We need to talk," he said.

Nine

Matt cursed under his breath. The look on Lauren's face told him all he needed to know.

She looked betrayed, angry and hurt. And she had every right to. But he'd never meant to hurt her, and the realization he'd caused her pain stabbed him like a knife.

"How did you get here?" she repeated.

He sighed as he reached her. "The valet pulled up with my car just a few minutes after I saw your cab pull away from the curb." He shrugged. "I left my brothers to deal with the security people back at the hotel."

He didn't add he'd driven with single-minded focus, guessing she was heading straight home.

"Let's go up and talk," he said.

"I've heard enough already," she retorted.

"The lobby will do," he countered, "but I'm not letting you stand out here in the cold."

"How nice of you to be concerned for my welfare," she responded acidly.

She turned and marched toward her building, using her key to open the front door.

Walking in behind her, he braked the door with his hand when she would have let it slam in his face.

She marched into the small reception area and turned to face him. "Say what you're going to say, and be quick about it."

He quirked an eyebrow at her strident tone, but decided it was best not to comment.

"On the night before the wedding, after the rehearsal dinner," he explained, "Parker and I wound up at the restaurant bar along with the other groomsmen."

She waited in tense silence for him to go on.

"We were the last two there, and I could tell something was up," Matt said. "Parker seemed jumpy, and after a few drinks, he wanted to talk. After listening to him for a while, I encouraged him to call off the wedding."

"So you don't deny it!"

"No, I don't. Parker was having doubts."

"And you encouraged him in those doubts," she accused.

"His doubts had a beginning and reality apart

from me," he countered. He had to make her see this.

"Parker is a weak guy," he went on. "He was getting married to please his powerful family, but when he finally realized you weren't exactly what they had in mind for a daughter-in-law, he concluded he'd rather be roaming the world as a free agent than settled down to domestic bliss."

He wasn't sugarcoating it for her. There was too much at stake, and he didn't want to lose her. If keeping her meant he had to paint Parker in all his unpretty stripes, then so be it. She'd had blinders on in that department for way too long anyway—it's what had almost gotten her to the altar.

"Not exactly what they had in mind?" she repeated. "You mean because my family isn't East Coat establishment, wealthy or well-known?"

He nodded. "You've got to have known Parker was putting up his share of the money for the wedding from his own pocket. His parents wanted nothing to do with putting together a rehearsal dinner where you'd be introduced to their friends and associates."

"Parker paid for the wedding because he could afford to," she said defiantly.

He shook his head. "And because his parents refused to."

"I suppose," she said acerbically, but still with an undertone of defiance, "they didn't expect Parker to present them with a woman he met during a party-hopping night on the town."

"You and Parker never really connected." He knew he had to tread carefully here. "In the bedroom, as well as out. You said as much yourself after our first time together."

"If you knew all these things about Parker, then why did you associate with him?" she retorted. "It seems to me you should have been spending your time warning the single women of Boston away from him."

He shrugged. "We were business school classmates, but we were never good buddies. I was asked to be a groomsman because I was a lucrative and powerful business contact. That's how things work in the world Parker's from."

"The world *you're* from."

Rather than deny it—he couldn't really deny it—he went on placatingly, "Encouraging Parker to listen to his doubts was the right thing to do. Would you rather have wound up in divorce court in a couple of years?"

"The right thing to do?" she repeated incredulously. "The night before my wedding?"

"Granted, the timing wasn't ideal."

"Now there's an understatement!" Her eyes flashed green fire. "Maybe by the night before the wedding, it would have been better to have just let Parker go through with it."

She paused for breath. "Maybe we would have found a way to work out any problems. How could you be sure we'd end up divorced? Are you omniscient or just arrogant?"

A muscle ticked in his jaw. "An interesting statement from a woman who makes her living predicting whether two people will be happy together."

"You're not the least bit sorry for your actions, are you?"

"I'm sorry you were hurt." It was the truth.

"You came to Ideal Match knowing, *knowing*, you'd had a hand in the whole wedding fiasco." Her brows snapped together. "When were you going to tell me?"

She raised a hand as if to stop his reply. "No, wait. I'm sure *not* before you talked me into going to bed with you."

"I may have made a mistake in judgment in that regard," he ground out. He didn't know how to placate her—how to reach her—at this point.

"No, *I* made a mistake," she contradicted, her eyes still snapping. "It was a mistake to take you on as a client, a mistake to get romantically involved with you, and a mistake to sleep with you."

His jaw hardened. "Like hell."

"I don't know what I was thinking. I compromised my professional principles, put Ideal Match's reputation on the line, and for what?"

"You were happy to book Boston's number one bachelor when you were focused on what it could mean for Ideal Match," he reminded her.

She opened her mouth, then clamped it shut. "You'd think I'd have learned from my experience with Parker not to get involved with anyone remotely associated with him."

"The fact you and Parker crashed and burned doesn't have anything to do with us."

"On the contrary," she argued, "it has everything to do with *us*. Or maybe I should say, there isn't any *us* anymore."

His eyes narrowed. "We could put the lie to those words."

"Yes, I forget you're Boston's most eligible man," she said, pausing meaningfully, "and destined to stay that way as far as I'm concerned."

He took two quick steps toward her, saw the flash of challenge in her eyes, and in the next instant, swept her into his arms.

He ravaged her mouth with his kiss, but underneath it was undeniable want and need.

They broke apart, and he took a step back, not trusting himself too close.

They were both breathing deeply.

"Is that the proof you were looking for?" she asked finally.

"What do you think?" he returned.

It had been plenty, and yet not nearly enough.

They stood there for a suspended moment that seemed to go on forever.

Then she turned and walked toward the elevator.

He watched her go, brooding as the elevator doors opened and she stepped inside.

She kept her face averted, not looking at him, as she punched a button and the elevator doors closed.

* * *

"I'm swearing off women," Matt found himself declaring.

"What?" Noah said disbelievingly. "Boston's Most Eligible Bachelor is going cold turkey off the world's most delectable dish? Say it ain't so."

It was Monday morning, and they were in Matt's office at Whittaker Enterprises. He was standing behind his desk, hands braced on hips, with documents his brother had just brought in arrayed before him.

Noah stood with arms crossed, but he still somehow appeared casual and relaxed.

Noah, Matt noted dryly, looked like a guy who'd spent the weekend having sex. *Unlike him.*

It had been two days since Saturday night's fiasco with Lauren, and he'd spent the weekend in a foul mood he'd carried into the office with him.

He shook his head at his brother. "I mean it. I just don't understand women."

Noah laughed. "Spoken just like a man in love. That's exactly what I said right before I realized I needed to propose to Kayla."

"You're nuts," he replied.

Noah was known as the family jokester, prone to making off-the-wall comments.

Besides, Matt thought, he felt like hell—worse than he'd ever felt over a woman—so it was unlikely he was mistaking one emotion for another.

"No, my friend, you're crazy," Noah said gravely. "Crazy in love, that is."

"Did you stop by to discuss work, or are you the firm's new resident psychologist?"

Noah gave a fleeting smile. "I came by to pay it forward. It's a family tradition."

"What?"

Noah shook his head. "Forget it. Let's just say Saturday night was the first time I've heard of you coming to blows with a guy over a woman. And not just any guy, either, but a man you were supposed to stand up for five years ago."

"Believe me, I'm not proud of it." As much as Parker had deserved it.

"It's not your usual style," Noah mused. "Most of the time, you're cool and unflappable."

He raked a hand through his hair. "My professional reputation is going to take a beating. I'm not even reading the newspaper headlines this morning."

He'd spent years cultivating the image of a cool enigma. He enjoyed keeping his business rivals off balance.

"I thought I was the family hothead," Noah quipped, "but you know, I'm glad to give up that title, too."

"Thanks a lot," he said sarcastically.

Noah tilted his head. "Lauren looked upset."

Upset was an understatement. He didn't like being reminded of the expression on Lauren's face. It had been a mixture of anxiety, hurt and surprise.

"But I can see why you were fighting over her."

Noah's expression turned to one of exaggerated lasciviousness. "Throw me some of *that* hot sauce."

His jaw hardened. "You're married."

"And you're not." Noah held up his hands, his eyes crinkling with amusement. "And hey, don't come after me now. I've seen the damage you CFO types can do with your right hook."

Matt grumbled. Noah's joking had a way of being right on target, as well as containing just the appropriate edge for its intended target.

Aloud, he said, "She told me to kiss off."

Noah grinned. "In your immortal words to me during my own hour of need, *resistance is futile.*"

Later, when Noah had left, Matt let himself dwell on what his brother had said. Was he in love with Lauren?

He sat back in his chair. He'd been reluctant to let his mind wander in that direction because it was a slippery slope to other, less comfortable revelations about himself.

He'd always thought—and still believed—he'd done the right thing when Parker had voiced doubts on the eve of the wedding. He'd never let himself question the purity of his motives.

But now he knew he wanted Lauren for himself, he'd opened the door to the question of *how long* he'd desired her.

Forever.

The response popped into his head.

He steepled his fingers. She'd taught him communication was the key to a good relationship, but was she ready to know what he really wanted?

"We're ruined."

Or rather, *she* was, Lauren thought.

"Oh, please." Candace rolled her eyes.

"*Yes.*"

It was Monday morning, and they were sitting in her office at Ideal Match. She'd called Candace to an emergency meeting—business, personal and plain girlfriend-to-girlfriend.

"*Au contraire,*" Candace replied. "This is the best thing that could have happened to Ideal Match. You had two eligible and socially prominent guys coming to blows over you. As far as the single women of Greater Boston are concerned, you're golden. They'll be beating a path to your door."

"At the moment, the only people beating a path to my door are reporters, and they're calling for a comment on Saturday's incident."

She couldn't bring herself to call it something more specific, though *incident* barely sufficed. Fight? Clash? Brawl?

She winced.

"Well, perhaps it was the *second best* thing that could have happened to Ideal Match," Candace allowed. "You know, after getting Matthew Whittaker hitched, preferably to yourself."

Now it was her turn to roll her eyes. "Haven't you heard anything I've said?"

She'd given Candace a rundown on the events leading up to the—her mind hiccupped again—*incident*. She'd relayed Parker's accusation, Matt's response, and then, later, Matt's refusal to say he'd done anything wrong.

"All right, what Matt did was fiendish," Candace conceded, "but would you want to be married to Parker right now? After hearing you describe his appearance on Saturday night—and I wish I'd been there to see it myself—I think you should be glad you dodged that bullet."

She shook her head in disbelief. "I can't believe you're going so soft on Matt."

"Any guy who's clued in enough to buy expensive jewelry qualifies for the highest rating in my book."

She'd forgotten about the necklace and earrings during her confrontation with Matt. There was no way she could keep them, however. "They're going back."

Candace looked at her in confusion for a second. "What? The diamonds?"

"Yes."

Candace stared at her in disbelief. "You're kidding."

"No."

"Well, that speaks volumes."

"What?" She couldn't help asking, even though she knew she wouldn't like the answer.

"You pawned Parker's engagement ring—which was a fitting price for him to pay for what he put you through, by the way—but you're sending the diamonds back to Matt. Now who's letting Matt off easy?"

"In the first place," she said, "Parker didn't ask for the ring back. I didn't even know where he was."

"Globe-trotting for pleasure and business apparently," Candace responded. "And anyway, I didn't hear anything about Matt asking for the jewelry back. Or did I miss something?"

"In the second place," she went on, not acknowledging Candace's point, "I ended the relationship, and I don't want to feel indebted to Matt in any way."

"Well, the fact he went to the trouble of selecting diamonds for you says something, doesn't it?"

"He learned something from being a client?"

Candace shook her head. "For one thing, he put himself on the line in order to make your fashion show a success."

"It was a brilliant marketing plan for getting him in front of appropriate women," she countered.

"He made you a priority," Candace replied. "He even agreed to meet you at home just so—"

"—yes, at *my* apartment, where he proceeded to—" She shut her mouth. Her receptionist wasn't supposed to know about what had transpired that evening.

Candace grinned wickedly. "Use the seductive arts you were supposed to be schooling him in?"

"No comment." She'd been saying it a lot this morning—to reporters, clients, associates and assorted gossips.

Candace got up to leave. "So if the guy shows up with an abject apology, you'll have him back, right?"

"Since the chances of Matt doing that are nil, it's a moot point."

"Still," her receptionist said, before her eyes came to rest on the questionnaire sitting before Lauren on her desk. "What's that?"

"Umm…" Lauren felt a flush creep up her face. She'd been contemplating Matt's answers to Ideal Match's questionnaire—the one he'd been filling out that first day in her office—before Candace had walked in.

Candace plucked the paper off her desk before she could stop her. "Mmm." She looked at Lauren and pursed her lips. "Matthew Whittaker's dossier. Let's see now."

Lauren sighed.

"I won't even ask why this is on your desk," Candace said, eyeing her.

Lauren felt heat rise to her face again. The truth was, she'd been torturing herself, trying to decipher Matt's answers, as if they held the key to the man— as if they might divulge hints of his past betrayal and general lack of trustworthiness.

Candace suddenly laughed and lowered the questionnaire. "Well, it's obvious why you couldn't match him. He was looking for you!"

She shot her receptionist a look of disbelief.

Candace dropped the paper on her desk. "Take

another look. It's not just the physical stuff, it's everything. *You're his fantasy.*"

She eyed the questionaire with a skeptical eye.

As Candace walked out of the room, she added, "Anybody can see you're perfect for each other."

Lauren closed her eyes and leaned her head back against her chair.

She'd put up a combative front for Candace, but the truth was, she was sick at heart.

She should be in bed right now with the shades drawn and the door shut. She should be eating ice cream straight from the tub and weeping over Humphrey Bogart's goodbye to Ingrid Bergman in *Casablanca.*

There was nothing like a classic heartbreak flick to let a woman drown in her sorrows.

Except she wasn't *only* a woman who wallowed in pain. On a couple of memorable occasions—her wedding day, the night of the Gala—she'd shown grit. At her wedding reception, she'd gyrated on the dance floor to Gloria Gaynor's "I Will Survive."

Her thoughts went back to Candace's words. For sure, Candace was wrong about the questionnaire.

Or maybe not.

Even in her pain, her heart wanted to believe….

She replayed Saturday night in her mind for the umpteenth time, stopping the video tape at key moments.

Yes, Matt had been wrong not to tell her about his

conversation with Parker, but the bottom line was, he'd done her a favor.

Now that her temper had cooled, she had to admit Candace was right. She was so much better off *not* being married to Parker.

Maybe she and Parker would still have been married today, but more likely not. And in the end, did it really matter? There was a good chance they'd have been unhappy even if they'd managed to remain married. She could see that now, from the man Parker had become—and the woman she'd become.

She thought again about Matt. He'd laid down his ego for her. He'd risked teasing from his brothers and raised eyebrows from others in order to help her with the Operatic League benefit. He'd taken a crash course in the techniques of Swedish massage. He'd brought food for Felix. And with varying levels of resistance, he'd let her redo his apartment and make him over.

Most importantly, he'd taught her how to fully experience true passion.

She had to give him a chance to explain—really explain—why he hadn't told her about his conversation with Parker. And even if the explanation wasn't convincing, she at least needed to have him see her perspective on the issue.

Because in the end, she had no choice. Because in the end, she still loved him.

Ten

"Well, see you Monday," Candace called on her way out the door, "and don't do anything I wouldn't do."

Lauren tried for a nonchalant smile. "Small chance of that."

"Oh, I don't know—" Candace winked "—recently you've had a wilder life than I have."

When the door closed behind Candace, Lauren was faced with the hushed emptiness of Ideal Match's office.

She thought about the diamond necklace and earrings in a locked drawer of her desk. Her plan was to hand deliver them to Matt after work today.

She'd told herself it was the most logical way to

get expensive jewels back to him, but in her heart, she knew her primary motivation was something else. If she deceived herself into thinking she was only going to return the jewelry, however, it was easier to find the courage to show up on his doorstep.

In fact, the only thing that had kept her away up to now was figuring out exactly what she'd say to him.

She hadn't told Candace about her plan for the evening because she knew her receptionist would jump to conclusions. Of course, perhaps that was why Candace had felt free to schedule a new client for her for the end of the day.

She sighed. With any luck, this meeting would be quick, and then she could get out of here to see Matt.

Itching for something to do while she waited, she gave in to temptation and retrieved his jewelry from her locked desk.

She touched the necklace with her fingertips, thinking back to how she'd felt when she'd first received it.

Overwhelmed. Emotions had bubbled up inside her, one after another.

Not giving herself time to think, she put the necklace and earrings on. It might be the last chance she had to wear them.

In some pitiable way, looking at them and trying them on when alone this week had made her feel closer to Matt. She recalled the look in his eyes when she'd paired them with the green gown, and her pulse fluttered.

A sudden sound from the reception area alerted her to the arrival of the last client of the day. Darn.

Candace must have left instructions with the security desk downstairs to allow up their after-hours visitor.

She looked down at herself. She supposed she didn't look too odd wearing a diamond necklace and earrings with a wool skirt and a V-neck blouse. And anyway, she really didn't have time to fiddle with taking off the jewelry.

She walked into the reception room, and came to a dead halt, her heart skipping a beat.

Matt.

They stared at each other for a moment.

As usual, he looked gorgeous, though a little windblown.

Still, after a beat, she noticed the shadows under his eyes and the deeper grooves around his mouth. He looked tired or sleep deprived, or maybe both.

He looked like she felt.

"What are you doing here?" she blurted.

She thought frantically about the jewelry at her ears and neck. Why hadn't she taken them off? Why had she taken them out?

Maybe he wouldn't notice. How could he *not* notice?

It would be hard to believe her now if she said she'd been planning to return the jewelry to him— because if she couldn't have him, she didn't want anything.

Maybe he'd think she was going to pawn the jewelry, she thought miserably, just as she'd done with her engagement ring.

"I've got an appointment," he said, and dumped the coat he was holding onto a nearby chair, seemingly unaware of her turmoil.

Suddenly, two thoughts came together. "You're the person Candace booked for six o'clock?"

"The one and only."

She thought back to Candace's vague and obfuscating answers to her questions about the new client scheduled for the end of the day:

"He called when you were out earlier this week," Candace had said breezily. "Sorry I forgot to mention it before now, but later today was the only time he could do."

She and Candace definitely needed to talk about office procedure, Lauren thought dimly. Specifically, they needed to address the issue of booking former lovers for appointments without letting the boss know.

"I've been thinking about what I'm looking for in a woman, and I have a better idea." He paused. "My requirements have changed a bit."

Her spirits sank, and she rushed to protect her vulnerable heart. "Lovely. And what does this have to do with me?"

He arched a brow. "You're still in the matchmaking business, aren't you? I thought getting Boston's number one bachelor married off was your big goal."

It had been. Once.

"If the past holds true," he went on, "I should be named the *Sentinel*'s Most Eligible Bachelor again any day now."

"I thought you wanted to find Ms. Right before that could happen," she countered.

His lips quirked. "This shouldn't take long. I've clarified what I'm looking for."

He was asking her to help him find her replacement? His nerve left her breathless. She couldn't believe he was here, let alone asking her to work for him again.

She was so caught off guard, however, and still worried about the jewelry—though he appeared not to have noticed it—that all she could think of doing was retreating to the familiar. "All right, let me get a pad."

It was just possible he thought he was doing her a favor. After all, staging a coup for Ideal Match *had been* high on her priority list.

But not now. Her mind fled back to nights of pure passion, tangled sheets and soft moans.

Forcing her thoughts back to the issue at hand, she walked to the reception desk on rubbery legs and fumbled for a pad and pen. "Okay, what are you looking for?"

"Down-to-earth," he responded resolutely.

"Yes, you said that before."

"Petite."

She frowned. "You already indicated you'd be open to the possibility."

"More than open," he said. "It's what I'm looking for."

She gave him a skeptical look.

He shrugged. "I like the height difference and the...compactness."

She jotted. "Anything else?"

She was willing to play along with his game, because the sooner she got him out of here, the better. Then she could go home and have herself a good cry.

"Yes." He took a step closer. "I like long hair."

"Many men prefer long hair."

"Count me among them," he said, "and among those who prefer green-eyed brunettes."

She thought back to the women she'd tried to set him up with who'd had that coloring. He'd rejected them both. Then she thought again about what Candace had said, and shied away from the thought.

He looked around. "Can we sit down?"

"Of course." She was stuck in professional gear, even as her mind shrieked this was so much more.

She walked over to the couch and sat down.

After taking a seat next to her, he turned toward her and leaned forward to rest his elbows on his legs and clasp his hands between them. "I'm looking for a woman who can handle some business entertaining, preferably while looking spectacular in a green satin gown."

Her hand skittered across the page, but after a moment, she picked up writing where she'd left off.

"Someone who's kind but ambitious." He smiled briefly. "Entrepreneurial, let's say, and maybe with her own business already."

She scribbled, not knowing what she was writing.

"Someone with some fashion and decorating sense, who can compensate for my shortcomings there."

She kept her eyes on the pad in front of her. Her heart beat so loudly, she was sure he could hear it.

"I want a woman softhearted enough to adopt a cat from a shelter but steely enough to handle me."

He reached out and removed the pad and paper from her nerveless fingers. "I want a woman," he said in a low voice, "who's dealt with life's setbacks and come out on top despite them."

He cupped her shoulders and turned her toward him, forcing her to look directly at him. "I want a woman who's terrific in bed—a woman who turns me on just by walking in the room. I'd *love* a woman like that."

She felt sluggish even as the blood roared in her ears.

He looked at her with glittery, hooded eyes. "I do love her."

His lips came down on hers, and he molded her mouth with his.

Her lips parted to give him entry, and the kiss turned deep and searching.

When he finally lifted his head, he said simply, "Marry me."

A wave of longing washed over her, turning her

insides to mush. She'd wanted him so badly and had missed him so much this past week.

"Marry me, and let's raise Felix together."

A strangled laugh escaped her even as she choked up. "I felt betrayed and deceived by you. It hurt more than what Parker did."

He nodded. "When I realized you were more upset with me than you were at Parker, I was betting it was because you cared more." He smiled. "Well, *that* and what Candace said."

"What *exactly* did Candace say?"

His eyes crinkled with amusement. "Just that you were lonesome and sad this week—"

Her eyes widened.

"—and that she was glad I called with a plan to show up on your doorstep, because in her opinion, I should get my butt over here pronto if I was tired of waiting for the rest of my life to get started."

She tilted her head. "Why did I ever think you were clueless about women?"

"Just where you're concerned," he corrected. "I got tongue-tied and brooding."

"Tongue-tied, you?" she teased. "Matt Whittaker, corporate titan?"

"I didn't want to screw things up, but I wound up doing it anyway."

She shook her head. "No, they turned out just right."

His expression turned serious. "I made an error in judgment. For starters, I should have told you when I first came into your office about my conversation with Parker on the night before the wedding. I should have let Parker come to his own decision about calling off the wedding."

"He would have made a lousy husband. I can admit that to myself now."

Of course, it was possible Parker would have been a different person today if their wedding had gone on as planned, but she doubted it.

"The thing is," Matt went on, "if I'd admitted to acting badly, I would also have had to face the reason why."

She gave him an inquiring look.

"And the reason is that I'm attracted to you." He paused significantly. "I've been attracted to you since the moment we met, but you were Parker's fiancée, and I needed to stay away."

"You acted as if you didn't even like me," she said. "I thought you were cold and aloof."

He gave her a self-deprecating look. "It keeps my business rivals on their toes. But with you, there was a guilty attraction, and the last thing I wanted was for you to guess it."

She felt full to bursting with emotion.

"I purposely made your job difficult," he admitted. "I started rejecting match after potential match because the only woman I wanted was you. At some point I realized I should have told you what happened with Parker, but the stakes were too high. I didn't want to risk driving you away."

"I was knocked over by Parker's charm and sophistication and wealth," she responded. "The relationship had problems, but I refused to see them."

"You found it easy to resist my charms," he teased.

She shook her head. "No, I couldn't resist, and that's what tied me up in knots. I thought I knew better now. When I met Parker, I was still a die-hard romantic who was eager to walk down the aisle. I saw him as my knight in shining armor."

Matt arched a brow. "His left hook is too puny to make him anyone's knight. The armor's rusty, too."

She gave a quivery laugh. "I was naive."

"You were beautiful," he countered.

She blinked away sudden tears. She'd turned a blind eye to signs of Parker's wishy-washiness. He hadn't been the settling-down, long-term commitment type, particularly with a nobody from the Sacramento suburbs.

But even worse, she'd compounded her mistake by attributing to Matt the characteristics she'd discerned about Parker.

What had Matt said? *I don't want to date women you think Parker would have liked to marry.* She winced thinking of how accurate the accusation had been.

Matt was witty and amusing, smart and socially adept, and willing to take risks for the woman he wanted. He was baring his soul to her and revealing his hidden heart. He was all she could hope for, and then some.

"You're all I ever wanted," she said, her voice full of unshed tears.

"In that case," he responded with amusement, "I hope you like this." He fished in his pocket.

She gasped when he pulled out a small velvet box and opened it to reveal a filigreed band with a large oval diamond.

His eyes twinkled. "It should go with the earrings and necklace you're wearing."

She felt herself flush. So he *had* noticed! "I was planning to return those to you. Tonight."

He tilted his head inquiringly.

"Actually, it was an excuse to come see you," she said. "I—I was really hoping we could work things out."

A slow grin spread across his face. "I'm a fan of kissing and making up."

"Yes." Her voice broke as she said it.

He nodded at the ring. "It's a Whittaker family heirloom. It's a platinum band worn by my great-grandmother. I had it cleaned up by the jewelers. That's why I held off on coming to see you. You deserved a proper proposal, even if—" he smiled wryly "—you wound up throwing the ring in my face."

She felt the tears well as he got down on one knee.

"Lauren, do you love me?"

"Yes," she warbled.

"Good. I was betting Candace wasn't wrong."

She sniffled. "I don't know whether to fire or promote Candace."

"Promote," he said emphatically. "That woman has the skills to be a first-class matchmaker."

She gave a tremulous smile.

His face got serious. "*Will* you marry me?"

"Yes, of course!"

He looked relieved—as if, she thought, there could be any doubt!

He slipped the ring onto her finger, then tossed the empty box onto a nearby chair.

He rose, and she stood, too.

"I love you," she said, pulling his head down to hers.

She'd never been happier, and with her newfound happiness came a newfound confidence.

She kissed him with all the passion and love pent up within her, her fingers diving into his hair.

The kiss went on and on, seeking and tasting, giving and taking, until she was dizzy with desire.

He pulled his mouth from hers, and said thickly, "Someone could come in."

"No one will come," she responded in a low voice. "It's after-hours, and I'm not expecting anyone—" the look she swept him was pure need "—or anything except spectacular sex."

"I've created a sex fiend," he murmured.

She gave him a wicked smile and went to work on his belt.

He shrugged out of his suit jacket and let it fall to the floor, then worked on loosening his tie.

Once she would have worried—worried about

her performance and worried about measuring up—but not anymore. She was floating on a cloud powered by happy air.

"Hurry," she urged, then stifled a giggle at his look of male frustration mixed with explosive desire.

"Okay, that's it," he growled, his control seeming to come untethered.

He hoisted her, and she wrapped her legs around him as he took three quick strides to Candace's desk.

She perched on the end of the wood surface, her skirt riding high on her thighs. The need to be joined to him was a palpable ache.

He looked like a man on the edge. His jaw etched in stone, his eyes bright and dark.

He gave her a quick, hard kiss, and she leaned back, coming to rest on her elbows.

She heard a couple of heavy objects fall off the desk and clatter to the floor. A stapler? A tape dispenser?

Matt pulled at the zipper of her knee-high black leather boots, and she was turned on by the sight of his hands on the butter-soft leather.

"Leave them," she said breathlessly.

"Yes," he said in husky agreement, then reached beneath her skirt to grasp her underwear and pull it off.

She sat up enough to pull her sweater over her head, baring her lacy bra to his gaze.

Then somehow he was between her legs again. His shirt hung open, his pants undone, his tie hanging loose around his neck.

She grasped the dangling ends of his tie and used it to pull him down toward her.

He took a moment to undo the front clasp of her bra, allowing her breasts to spring free so he could nuzzle and kiss them, before his mouth returned to hers.

There would be no barrier between them this time, she thought. They'd shared information about their sexual histories, and now, they'd opened up to each other in an even more profound way.

"You could get pregnant," he muttered, as if reading her mind.

"Your questionnaire said you wanted kids," she said simply.

His expression heated. "Yes, with you."

He took his time to ready her with his hand, then he slid into her, filling her.

She closed her eyes and moaned.

Bliss.

He began to move inside her, and she helped him shift her to a better position.

She clung to him as they climbed, the world closing in around them, nothing but the sweet sensation between them existing, until finally she felt as if she was at the edge of the precipice.

Matt groaned. "Come on, honey."

It was the last encouragement she needed before she went up and over, flying across the void to sweet release.

He followed her a moment later, pulling her tight to him and finding his release.

It was ecstasy, it was everything. Today was the start of the rest of their lives and she couldn't wait for the rest to unfold.

"I love you," she said.

"Likewise, sweetheart." He kissed her nose. "Likewise."

Epilogue

Life was good. Matt looked around him. It was the annual Memorial Day weekend barbecue at his parents' sprawling home, and the Whittakers had come full circle.

Several years before, his sister-in-law Elizabeth had come to the barbecue, planning to have a baby on her own by using a sperm donor. Before anyone could blink, though, Elizabeth had become pregnant with Quentin's baby. Their son had been born early the following year—the first Whittaker grandbaby.

Matt looked over at his brother and sister-in-law, who were talking with another couple under the shade of an oak tree in the Whittakers' backyard. They'd been married over five years now and still looked unbelievably happy. Elizabeth's design business continued to thrive, though she'd hired a couple of employees and scaled back on her own involvement since she'd had kids. And despite all odds, Elizabeth had become pregnant again and had recently given birth to baby Sophia.

Actually, Matt thought, the Whittakers had experienced something of a baby boom lately.

Allison had given birth last year to now fifteen-month-old Will. His sister was using her experience as a public prosecutor as a consultant for her husband's security business.

In the next moment, Matt caught sight of Noah. Now *that* had been a surprise. Once perceived as the playboy Whittaker, Noah was now the father of one-year-old twins, Ella and Jake. Kayla, who was now freelancing for the *Boston Sentinel*, swore she never thought she'd see the day when Noah would be spending his time playing with dolls and building blocks.

"Why are you smiling?"

Matt grinned as he watched his wife toddle over to him. "Hey, you."

At seven months pregnant, Lauren radiated happiness from the inside out.

The sonogram she'd had in her fifth month had shown they were expecting a boy, and they'd already settled on the name Fletcher, Lauren's maiden name.

"You didn't answer my question," Lauren said as he draped an arm over her shoulders and pulled her close.

"Just thinking about us Whittakers." He glanced around and then down at her. "A few years ago, we would have been prime candidates for Ideal Match. Now look at us."

"And who do you guys have to thank for that?"

Matt glanced up to see Allison and Connor, who was holding Will, stroll up to join them.

"Hmm, let's see." He pretended to consider before asking skeptically, "You?"

"That's right, big brother." Allison nodded approvingly. "You may have been the last Whittaker standing, but you shouldn't have thought for a minute that the rest of us would let you off the hook."

"Let Matt off the hook for what?" Noah asked as he and Quentin and their wives walked up to them, kids in tow.

"For being the last Whittaker not married," Allison replied.

Adjusting Sophia into his arms, Quent said, "That's right, Matt. Did you really think Allison would rest before she got you hooked up?"

Matt quirked a brow. "All she did was suggest I hire a matchmaker."

"Not just any matchmaker," Allison corrected. "Lauren Fletcher of Ideal Match."

He groaned. "Don't tell me it was a deliberate choice."

"Okay, I won't," Allison said sweetly, and everyone else laughed.

Sometimes his sister confounded him, Matt thought. "How could you have known?"

"For starters, Lauren was—*is*—one of the best," Allison responded.

Well, that was true. Though Lauren had recently taken on Candace as a partner and had hired a sassy new receptionist, Matt knew she wanted to keep a hand in the development of her business. She was, in fact, planning to write a book based on her experiences as Dr. Date.

"Second," Allison went on, "I knew Lauren had once been engaged to your old classmate Parker, and I remember you got rather tight-lipped, Matt, right around the time the newspapers reported the wedding had been called off."

"And from that flimsy evidence you deduced Lauren and I were soul mates destined to spend our lives together?" he asked skeptically.

Allison smiled placidly. "No, I didn't go that far, but I thought it might be interesting to see what happened when the two of you were thrown back together."

"*Interesting?*" he echoed. "That's putting it mildly."

"Exactly. Sparks flew—" Allison held out her hands "—and look at you now."

He couldn't argue there.

Allison shrugged. "Besides, getting Kayla to have you named the *Sentinel*'s Most Eligible Bachelor wasn't working."

"You did that?" He looked from his sister to his sister-in-law and then back.

"Well…" Allison hedged, seemingly belatedly realizing she might have revealed too much.

"You *are* devious," he said with disbelief.

All the women laughed.

He looked down at Lauren. "You approve?"

"Who am I to judge?" Lauren responded laughingly. "I make my living trying to set people up. Besides, I got you, didn't I?"

He gave her an over-the-top look. "Oh, you've got me."

"Okay, okay, break it up," Noah put in.

"Anyway, Matt," Allison said, a note of suspicion in her voice, "we're still wondering whether you didn't plot and plan your way to being the last available Whittaker."

"Yeah," Noah seconded. "You were always the quiet one. Still waters run deep, and all that jazz."

He allowed an enigmatic smile to spread across his face. He'd had enough teasing. "You'll just have to accept that some things are destined to remain a mystery."

Lauren looked from her husband to the family around her, and basked in the easy camaraderie.

When she'd first moved to Boston, she'd never dreamed she'd find herself here. She was glad now she'd stuck it out.

Matt had awakened a part of her that had been dormant for five years. She felt more alive now, less fearful and more willing to experience the moment fully.

She smiled up at Matt. Who'd ever have thought her tight-lipped CFO would be the man who drew her out of herself? She couldn't have imagined it when he'd walked into her office.

Months after he proposed, they'd had a beautiful October wedding. It had been an Indian summer day, and the leaves had been changing color.

The wedding had been relatively small, rather than the society hoopla her first was to have been, and it had gone off without a hitch. All of their siblings and spouses, as well as a jubilant Candace, had been in the wedding party. The Whittakers and the Fletchers had taken to each other like ducks to water, and she and Matt had wound up honeymooning at a private compound in Fiji.

What's more, getting married had made her even better at her job. Thanks to her own experience, she was more intuitive when it came to figuring out what her clients needed and who would be an ideal match.

"That smile must mean something," Matt said.

"Uh-oh, the newlyweds are at it again," Noah interjected.

Because she and Matt were the couple who'd married most recently, they were still referred to as newlyweds by the rest of the Whittakers.

"I'm just happy," she said.

She still got a thrill from thinking of Matt as her

husband. And even at seven months pregnant, he made her feel sexy.

Matt lowered his head and gave her a quick kiss that was full of promise. *Later,* his eyes said as he raised his head. *There'll be more later. I promise.*

She watched then as he looked around and said, "Everyone grab a drink."

Matt grabbed a beer for himself and handed her a glass of flavored water.

After a moment, he raised his hand in a toast. "To us, Whittakers, because we each found our ideal match."

There were murmurs of agreement as everyone raised their glass before tasting their drinks.

Then Matt leaned in for a kiss, and the last thing Lauren saw before she closed her eyes was the sweetest image of all: the man to whom she'd given her heart, and who loved her with all his heart in return.

* * * * *

Happily ever after is just the beginning...

Turn the page for a sneak preview of
DANCING ON SUNDAY AFTERNOONS
by
Linda Cardillo

*Harlequin Everlasting—Every great love has
a story to tell. ™*
*A brand-new line from Harlequin Books
launching this February!*

Prologue

Giulia D'Orazio
1983

I had two husbands—Paolo and Salvatore.

Salvatore and I were married for thirty-two years. I still live in the house he bought for us; I still sleep in our bed. All around me are the signs of our life together. My bedroom window looks out over the garden he planted. In the middle of the city, he coaxed tomatoes, peppers, zucchini—even grapes for his wine—out of the ground. On weekends, he used to drive up to his cousin's farm in Waterbury and bring back manure. In the winter, he wrapped the peach tree and the fig tree with rags and black rubber hoses against the cold, his massive, coarse hands gentling those trees as if they were his fragile-skinned babies. My neighbor, Dominic Grazza, does that for me now. My boys have no time for the garden.

In the front of the house, Salvatore planted roses. The roses I take care of myself. They are giant, cream-colored, fragrant. In the afternoons, I like to sit out on the porch with my coffee, protected from the eyes of the neighborhood by that curtain of flowers.

Salvatore died in this house thirty-five years ago. In the last months, he lay on the sofa in the parlor so he could be in the middle of everything. Except for the two oldest boys, all the children were still at home and we ate together every evening. Salvatore could see the dining room table from the sofa, and he could hear everything that was said. "I'm not dead, yet," he told me. "I want to know what's going on."

When my first grandchild, Cara, was born, we brought her to him, and he held her on his chest, stroking her tiny head. Sometimes they fell asleep together.

Over on the radiator cover in the corner of the parlor is the portrait Salvatore and I had taken on our twenty-fifth anniversary. This brooch I'm wearing today, with the diamonds—I'm wearing it in the photograph also—Salvatore gave it to me that day. Upstairs on my dresser is a jewelry box filled with necklaces and bracelets and earrings. All from Salvatore.

I am surrounded by the things Salvatore gave me, or did for me. But, God forgive me, as I lie alone now in my bed, it is Paolo I remember.

Paolo left me nothing. Nothing, that is, that my family, especially my sisters, thought had any value. No house. No diamonds. Not even a photograph.

But after he was gone, and I could catch my breath from the pain, I knew that I still had something. In the middle of the night, I sat alone and held them in my hands, reading the words over and over until I heard his voice in my head. I had Paolo's letters.

* * * * *

Be sure to look for
DANCING ON SUNDAY AFTERNOONS
available January 30, 2007.
And look, too, for our other Everlasting title
available,
FALL FROM GRACE by Kristi Gold.

FALL FROM GRACE is a deeply emotional story
of what a long-term love really means.
As Jack and Anne Morgan discover,
marriage vows can be broken—but they
can be mended, too.
And the memories of their marriage have
an unexpected power
to bring back a love that never really left....

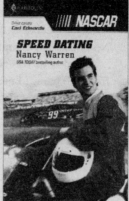
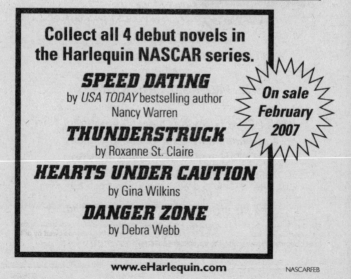

REQUEST YOUR FREE BOOKS!

2 FREE NOVELS PLUS 2 FREE GIFTS!

Passionate, Powerful, Provocative!

SDES06

HARLEQUIN®

Super Romance®

Is it really possible to find true love
when you're single...with kids?

Introducing an exciting new five-book miniseries,

SINGLES...WITH KIDS

When Margo almost loses her bistro...and custody of
her children...she realizes a real family is about more
than owning a pretty house and being a perfect mother.
And then there's the new man in her life, Robert...
Like the other single parents in her support group, she
has to make sure he wants the whole package.

Starting in February 2007 with

LOVE AND THE SINGLE MOM

by C.J. Carmichael

(Harlequin Superromance #1398)

ALSO WATCH FOR:

THE SISTER SWITCH Pamela Ford (#1404, on sale March 2007)
ALL-AMERICAN FATHER Anna DeStefano (#1410, on sale April 2007)
THE BEST-KEPT SECRET Melinda Curtis (#1416, on sale May 2007)
BLAME IT ON THE DOG Amy Frazier (#1422, on sale June 2007)

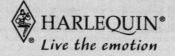

HARLEQUIN®
Live the emotion

www.eHarlequin.com   HSRLSM0207

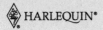

HARLEQUIN®

EVERLASTING LOVE™

Every great love has a story to tell™

Save $1.⁰⁰ off

**the purchase of
any Harlequin
Everlasting Love novel**

Coupon valid from January 1, 2007
until April 30, 2007.

Valid at retail outlets in the U.S. only.
Limit one coupon per customer.

5 65373 00076 2   (8100) 0 11302

HEUSCPN0407

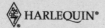

EVERLASTING LOVE™

Every great love has a story to tell™

Fall from Grace

Kristi Gold

Save $1.⁰⁰ off

the purchase of
any Harlequin
Everlasting Love novel

Coupon valid from January 1, 2007
until April 30, 2007.

Valid at retail outlets in Canada only.
Limit one coupon per customer.

52607370

HECDNCPN0407

HARLEQUIN® *Romance*®

What a month!

In February watch for

Rancher and Protector
Part of the Western Weddings miniseries
BY JUDY CHRISTENBERRY

The Boss's Pregnancy Proposal
BY RAYE MORGAN

Also in February, expect
MORE of what you love
as the Harlequin Romance line
increases to six titles per month.

Don't miss the first book
in THE ROYALS trilogy:

THE FORBIDDEN PRINCESS
(SD #1780)

by national bestselling author

DAY LECLAIRE

Moments before her loveless royal wedding,
Princess Alyssa was kidnapped by a mysterious man
who'd do anything to stop the ceremony. Even if that
meant marrying the forbidden princess himself!

On sale February 2007 from Silhouette Desire!

THE ROYALS
Stories of scandals and secrets
amidst the most powerful palaces.

Make sure to read the other titles in the series:
THE PRINCE'S MISTRESS
On sale March 2007
THE ROYAL WEDDING NIGHT
On sale April 2007

*Available wherever books are sold, including most
bookstores, supermarkets, discount stores and drugstores.*

Visit Silhouette Books at www.eHarlequin.com SDTFP0207